William Shakespeare's Romeo and Juliet: A Retelling in Prose

David Bruce

Published by David Bruce, 2022.

This is a work of fiction. Similarities to real people, places, or events are entirely coincidental.

WILLIAM SHAKESPEARE'S ROMEO AND JULIET: A RETELLING IN PROSE

First edition. July 28, 2022.

Copyright © 2022 David Bruce.

ISBN: 979-8201329693

Written by David Bruce.

Table of Contents

Dedication

Dedicated to Carl Eugene Bruce and Josephine Saturday Bruce

My father, Carl Eugene Bruce, died on 24 October 2013. He used to work for Ohio Power, and at one time, his job was to shut off the electricity of people who had not paid their bills. He sometimes would find a home with an impoverished mother and some children. Instead of shutting off their electricity, he would tell the mother that she needed to pay her bill or soon her electricity would be shut off. He would write on a form that no one was home when he stopped by because if no one was home he did not have to shut off their electricity.

The best good deed that anyone ever did for my father occurred after a storm that knocked down many power lines. He and other linemen worked long hours and got wet and cold. Their feet were freezing because water got into their boots and soaked their socks. Fortunately, a kind woman gave my father and the other linemen dry socks to wear.

My mother, Josephine Saturday Bruce, died on 14 June 2003. She used to work at a store that sold clothing. One day, an impoverished mother with a baby clothed in rags walked into the store and started shoplifting in an interesting way: The mother took the rags off her baby and dressed the infant in new clothing. My mother knew that this mother could not afford to buy the clothing, but she helped the mother dress her baby and then she watched as the mother walked out of the store without paying.

***

The doing of good deeds is important. As a free person, you can choose to live your life as a good person or as a bad person. To be a good person, do good deeds. To be a bad person, do bad deeds. If you do good deeds, you will become good. If you do bad deeds, you will become bad. To become the person you want to be, act as if you already are that kind of person. Each of us chooses what kind of person we will become. To become a good person, do the things a good person does. To become a bad person, do the things a bad person does. The opportunity to take action to become the kind of person you want to be is yours.

A Buddhist monk visiting a class wrote this on the chalkboard: "EVERYONE WANTS TO SAVE THE WORLD, BUT NO ONE

WANTS TO HELP MOM DO THE DISHES." The students laughed, but the monk then said, "Statistically, it's highly unlikely that any of you will ever have the opportunity to run into a burning orphanage and rescue an infant. But, in the smallest gesture of kindness — a warm smile, holding the door for the person behind you, shoveling the driveway of the elderly person next door — you have committed an act of immeasurable profundity, because to each of us, our life is our universe."

Cover Photograph for William Shakespeare's *Romeo and Juliet*: A Retelling in Prose:
Madalin Calita
Oltenita, Romania

Educate Yourself
Read Like A Wolf Eats
Be Excellent to Each Other
Books Then, Books Now, Books Forever

***

In this retelling, as in all my retellings, I have tried to make the work of literature accessible to modern readers who may lack some of the knowledge about mythology, religion, and history that the literary work's contemporary audience had.

Do you know a language other than English? If you do, I give you permission to translate this book, copyright your translation, publish or self-publish it, and keep all the royalties for yourself. (Do give me credit, of course, for the original retelling.)

I would like to see my retellings of classic literature used in schools, so I give permission to the country of Finland (and all other countries) to give copies of this book to all students forever. I also give permission to the state of Texas (and all other states) to give copies of this book to all students forever. I also give permission to all teachers to give copies of this book to all students forever.

Teachers need not actually teach my retellings. Teachers are welcome to give students copies of my books as background material. For example, if they are teaching Homer's *Iliad* and *Odyssey*, teachers are welcome to give students copies of my *Virgil's* Aeneid: *A Retelling in Prose* and tell students, "Here's another ancient epic you may want to read in your spare time."

CAST OF CHARACTERS

Juliet: Capulet's daughter

Romeo: Montague's son

Mercutio: Kinsman to the Prince of Verona and friend of Romeo

Tybalt: Lady Capulet's nephew and Juliet's cousin

The Nurse: Juliet's nursemaid

Friar Lawrence: A Franciscan, and Romeo's confessor

Capulet: Juliet's father

Paris: A noble kinsman to the Prince

Benvolio: Montague's nephew

Lady Capulet: Juliet's mother

Montague: Romeo's father

Balthasar: Romeo's servant

Apothecary: a chemist, aka pharmacist

Escalus: the Prince of Verona

Friar John: A Franciscan, friend to Friar Lawrence

Lady Montague: Romeo's mother

Peter: A Capulet servant attending the Nurse

Abram: A servant to Montague

Gregory and Sampson: Servants of the Capulet household

PROLOGUE

The Capulets and the Montagues — two families, very much alike in most respects — in the beautiful city of Verona, Italy, battle each other because of a long-standing feud. Because of this feud, the hands of the citizens of Verona become dirty with the blood of other citizens of Verona. The two families have given birth to two children — a boy named Romeo and a girl named Juliet — who become ill-fated lovers and commit suicide. The burial of these lovers also buries the quarrel between their two families. These lovers' story is told in this book.

CHAPTER 1: ROMEO AND JULIET MEET

— 1.1 —

On a street of Verona, Samson and Gregory, two servants of the Capulet family, walked and talked. They wore swords and carried small, round shields. Samson was in a mood to boast about his masculinity, and both were in a mood to make jokes.

Sampson said, "Gregory, you and I are not the type to take insults lightly."

Gregory replied, "Neither of us is a lightweight."

"If anyone should make us angry and choleric, we would draw our swords."

"I definitely recommend that you not be collared by the city guards."

Sampson said, "When I am moved by anger, I strike quickly with my sword."

Gregory replied, "True, but it is best to not be quickly moved to strike."

"Any member of the family of Montague can quickly move me to anger."

"To quickly move is to run. A courageous man will stand and face the enemy. Are you telling me that when you meet a Montague you will run away?"

Sampson said, "A male Montague will move me to anger and a female Montague will make a certain part of my body move to make a stand. If we meet a Montague man on the street, I will make the Montague man walk in the gutter while I walk next to this wall."

Gregory replied, "Doesn't that mean that you are weak? The weaker sex walks on the side away from the street while the stronger sex walks next to the street. Members of the weaker sex will walk next to this wall."

"You talk truthfully. Women are weak and need to be specially treated. If we meet a Montague man, I will push him into the gutter. But if we meet a Montague woman, I will nail her ass to this wall."

"This feud is between the heads of the Capulets and the Montagues. And yet, the feud extends between other members of the two families and even to servants such as us."

Sampson replied, "So be it. I will act like a tyrant. I will fight the Montague men, and then I will cruelly cut off the heads of the Montague maidens."

"The heads of the maidens?" Gregory asked.

"Yes, the heads of the maidens, or better, I will break their maidenheads. Take it either way, but while I am alive, let no Montague hymen be unbroken."

"If the Montague maidens take it, they will feel it inside them."

Sampson said, "I will stand and deliver. Part of me will stand up, and I will deliver it to the Montague maidens. What I will deliver to the Montague maidens is a pretty piece of flesh."

"It is good that you are flesh and not fish," Gregory said. "If you were fish, you would be dried fish — dried and shriveled up."

Gregory saw Abraham and Balthasar, two servants of the Montague family, and said to Samson, "Draw your sword. Here come two Montagues."

"My naked sword is out of its scabbard, but if these two Montagues were Montague women and not Montague men, my sword is not the naked tool I would now be displaying. Pick a quarrel with these Montagues — I have your back."

"In what way? Will you turn your back and run?"

"Don't worry."

"As long as I have *you* at my back, I worry."

Sampson said, "Let's not break the law. Let them start a quarrel."

"I will frown as I pass by them," Gregory said. "They can take it as they wish."

"That's not enough," Samson said. "I will rub my nose with my middle finger. If they don't start a fight, they will be thought to be cowardly."

As Abraham and Balthasar neared them, Samson pulled his fingers into a fist, extended his middle finger, and rubbed the tip of his nose while staring at the Montague servants.

Abraham asked angrily, "Are you giving us the finger?"

"I am indeed giving the finger," Samson replied.

"Yes, I can see that you are," Abraham said, "but are you giving *us* the finger?"

Samson asked Gregory, "Is the law on our side, if I say yes?"

"No," Gregory replied.

Samson said to the Montague servants, "No, I am not giving you the finger, but I am giving the finger."

Gregory said to the Montague servants, "Are you picking a fight with us?"

"A fight?" Abraham said. "No."

"If you want to fight, I will fight you," Sampson said. "My boss is as good as yours."

"He is no better," Abraham said.

Gregory said, "Say that our boss is better than his boss. I see a reinforcement coming: Benvolio, a relative of our boss."

"You are wrong," Samson said to Abraham. "Our boss is better than your boss."

"You lie!" Abraham shouted.

"Draw your swords if you are men," Sampson said. "Gregory, get ready to fight — you know how to cut and slash with your sword."

Benvolio, a peacemaker, drew his sword and tried to stop the fight. He shouted, "Part, fools! Put up your swords; you don't know what you do!" He used his sword to beat down their swords.

Tybalt, a Montague, came running with his sword drawn and said to Benvolio, "You have drawn your sword among these stupid servants. Turn, and face a worthy opponent. Turn, and face your death."

"I do but try to keep the peace," Benvolio said. "Put up your sword, or use it to help me separate these quarreling men."

"What! You have drawn your sword, and you are talking about being a peacekeeper!" Tybalt mocked. "I hate the word 'peace' as I hate Hell, all Montagues, and you. Let's fight, coward!"

Tybalt and Benvolio fought.

News of the fight spread quickly, and soon several Capulets and Montagues came running and started to fight. Some guards — officers of the law — also arrived.

A guard shouted, "Beat down the weapons of both the Capulets and the Montagues! Stop this fight!"

Old Capulet, the head of the Capulet family, heard the commotion. Still in his nightgown, he ran out of his house and shouted, "What noise is this? Give me my long sword!"

His much younger wife, Mrs. Capulet, said to him, "Why are you asking for a sword? You can get much more use out of a crutch!"

Old Capulet repeated, "Bring me my sword, I say! Old Montague has come, and he has drawn his blade in defiance of me."

Old Montague and his wife arrived on the scene. Old Montague shouted, "Old Capulet, you are a villain!"

His wife grabbed onto him. He shouted at her, "Hold me not! Let me go!"

She told him, "You shall not stir a foot to seek a foe."

The Prince of Verona and his armed bodyguards rode into the street. Prince Escalus wanted a peaceful city, and he was determined to have one, even if he had to threaten to torture and kill some people to get peace.

The Prince shouted, "Rebellious subjects, enemies to peace, you who coat your steel swords with your neighbors' blood, listen to me! Either throw your weapons to the ground or be sentenced to death by torture."

They threw down their weapons. The Prince was the ruler of the city, and if he ordered his bodyguards to kill someone, his bodyguards would instantly obey him.

The Prince continued, "Three brawls in the street have disturbed the peace of our city. Three brawls that were caused by words that dissipated into the air — words spoken by you, Old Capulet, and by you, Old Montague. Your airy words have caused you two old men of Verona to put aside your dignified and appropriate behavior and caused you to wield old weapons in your old hands. You are putting weapons that are rusty with peace and disuse in your arthritic hands to serve your hatred of each other. Listen to what I decree: If ever you or your families fight in our streets again, you will pay for your crime with your lives: If you fight, you die!

"Old Capulet, come with me now. Old Montague, come to me this afternoon. Meet me in old Freetown, the court where I make judgments.

"All of you, I order you to leave here. Leave peacefully and immediately, or die."

Everyone left. Old Montague, his wife, and Benvolio walked away slowly together.

Old Montague asked Benvolio, "What happened? Who caused this newest fight in our ancient feud? Were you here when it happened?"

"Before I arrived, servants of the Capulet family and servants of our family were already fighting," Benvolio said. "I drew my sword in an attempt to part them and reestablish the peace. But Tybalt of the Capulet family came running with his sword drawn. He shouted his hatred of me and other Montagues while he swung his sword around his head. His sword did not hurt the air, which hissed at him in scorn. Tybalt talks a good fight, but his talking is better than his fighting. He and I fought, and more and more people arrived and began fighting either for the Capulets or for our side. The Prince then arrived and stopped the fighting."

Mrs. Montague said, "Where is my son, Romeo? Have you seen him? I am glad that he was not fighting here."

"An hour before sunrise, I took a walk because my mind was troubled," Benvolio said. "I saw your son walking in a grove of sycamore trees to the West of the city. I was walking toward him, but he saw me and walked away. I could tell that he wished to be alone, as did I. I did not go to him."

Old Montague said, "Romeo has often been seen there before sunrise. His tears fall and are added to the morning dew. But as soon as the Sun begins to rise, my melancholy son returns home and shuts himself up alone in his room. He closes the windows and shuts out the sunlight, turning what should be a brightly lit room into an artificial night. His mood will stay black and ominous unless someone can find out what is bothering him."

"My noble uncle, do you know the cause of Romeo's depression?"

"I don't know the cause, and he won't tell me what is bothering him."

"Have you tried to find out?"

"Yes, I have asked him," Old Montague said. "So have many of my friends. But he keeps his thoughts private and won't talk to us. His depression is like a worm that bites the bud of a flower and keeps it from spreading its petals and displaying its beauty to the Sun. I want to know what is bothering him so I can fix the problem."

Benvolio said, "I see Romeo walking toward us now. Let me be alone with him. I will do everything I can to find out what is bothering him."

Old Montague replied, "Good luck. I hope that he tells you what is making him depressed."

He then said to his wife, "Let's go away and leave Benvolio and our son alone."

They left, and Benvolio walked toward Romeo.

"Good morning, Romeo," Benvolio said.

"Is it still morning?"

"The clock just now struck nine."

"Sad hours seem long," Romeo said. "Was that my father who left just now?"

"Yes, it was. What sadness makes your hours seem long?"

"My sadness is that I do not have the thing that if I had it would make my hours seem short."

"You sound as if you are in love," Benvolio said.

"Out —"

"Of love?"

"Out of the favor of the person I love."

"Being in love seems like a good thing, but all too often love is harsh."

"Love is supposed to be blind, but it has made me its bitch — so, where do you want to eat?"

Benvolio was wise enough not to smile, but he thought, *Romeo can't be very deeply in love if he can still think of his stomach instead of the woman who does not love him although he thinks he loves her.*

Romeo noticed blood on the ground and said, "Who has been fighting here? Don't tell me. I can guess. It's the feud. Here has been a battle among men who hate each other but love to fight each other. Here has been brawling love and loving hate. With these men, love and hate are entwined with each other. We might as well talk of creating something out of nothing! We might as well talk of heavy lightness and serious vanity! We might as well talk of beautiful forms that look ugly! We might as well talk of lead feathers and bright smoke and cold fire and sick health! We might as well talk of still-waking sleep. These fighting men know nothing of love. The love I feel makes me feel no love for this brawl.

"Benvolio, are you laughing at me?"

"No, Romeo. Instead, I weep."

"Why?"

"Because you are unhappy."

Romeo said, "Unhappiness is often the consequence of love. I have griefs to bear in my heart, and yet your grief becomes added to my griefs, although I already have too much grief to bear. What is love? Love is a smoke that rises with the sighs of lovers. When love is returned, you can see a fire burning in both lovers' eyes. When love is refused, a sea is created with the rejected lover's tears. What else is love? It is a most intelligent madness. It is a thing that chokes, and it is a thing that tastes sweet. Farewell, Benvolio."

"Wait!" Benvolio said. "I will go with you. If you leave me now, you do me wrong."

"I have lost myself," Romeo said. "I am not Romeo — he is some other where."

"Be serious," Benvolio said, "and tell me who it is you love."

"Shall I groan and tell you?"

"You need not groan," Benvolio said, "but be serious and do tell me who it is you love."

"'Serious' is a word that ought not to be used in front of a dying man who needs to make a will," Romeo said, "but seriously, Benvolio, I love a woman."

"When you said you loved someone, I did indeed think you loved a woman. I know you that well. Tell me more."

"When you thought I loved a woman, you hit a bull's-eye," Romeo said. "She is indeed beautiful."

"I have hit another bull's-eye," Benvolio said. "I also thought that she would be beautiful. If she is the target of your love, what kind of a marksman have you been?"

"The worst possible," Romeo replied. "She is a target who will not allow herself to be hit with the arrow of Cupid. She wants nothing to do with romantic love. She is a follower of Diana, a virgin goddess, and she wishes, like Diana, always to remain a virgin. She vigilantly defends her chastity and wears metaphorical armor that defends her body from the arrows of Cupid. She will not listen to loving compliments. She ignores loving looks. She will not open her lap to receive gifts of saint-seducing gold. She is rich with beauty, but when she dies her beauty will be buried with her."

"Then she has sworn always to remain a virgin?"

"She has, indeed," Romeo said, "and so she is wasting her beauty. By remaining forever a virgin, she will never give birth to a daughter who will inherit her beauty. She is too beautiful and too intelligent and too fashionable to be allowed into Paradise after refusing to return my love. She should not receive eternal bliss as a result of making me despair. She has sworn never to love, and that is something she should never have sworn. By doing so, she has killed the best part of me, leaving only a husk to tell you my story."

"Take my advice," Benvolio said. "Forget about her."

"Tell me how it is possible to do that."

"Simply allow your eyes to look at other beautiful women."

"If I do that, I will only remember the more her beauty," Romeo said. "At masked balls, women put masks over their face but we remember that beauty lies underneath the mask. A man who goes blind will still remember the beauty that he has seen. Show me a beautiful woman, and I will simply remember the woman I love — a woman who is more beautiful than any woman you show me. You cannot teach me how to forget my love, so farewell, Benvolio."

Romeo left, and Benvolio said, "You think I cannot teach how to forget your love, but I think I can."

He walked after Romeo.

In his mansion, Old Capulet was planning a party, one that he held annually. He also was hosting Count Paris. A relative of the Prince, Paris would be an important political ally if he would marry Juliet, Old Capulet's daughter. Paris had come to Old Capulet to see about arranging that marriage.

Old Capulet said to Paris, "I believe that the upcoming days will be peaceful. If I fight, I die. If Old Montague fights, he dies. With such a penalty over our heads, and with Montague and I being so old, it should not be hard for us to keep the peace."

"Both of you are honorable men of good reputation, and it is a pity that you have feuded," Paris said. "But will you allow me to marry your daughter, Juliet?"

"I can say only what I have said before," Old Capulet said. "My daughter is yet a stranger in the world — she is not yet fourteen years old. She will have to be sixteen before I can think of allowing her to get married."

Paris replied, "Younger than she are happy mothers made."

Thinking of his much younger wife, Old Capulet said, "And too soon marred are those so early made mothers. All of my other children are dead and buried; Juliet is my only child who is left alive. In her I place my hopes. But woo her, Paris, and win her heart. My consent to the marriage is only part of what is needed. If she agrees to the marriage, I will gladly give my consent.

"Today I am giving a party, one I hold each year. I have invited many guests whom I love, and I invite you to be a welcomed guest. Come to my house tonight. You will see young girls who will seem to be stars that walk on the Earth and light up the night sky from below. After the cold winter come warm April and many beautiful flowers. The young girls you see at my party tonight are as beautiful as April flowers — look at all of them and talk to all of them. Fall in love with the one whom you think most deserves your love. That one may be my daughter, or perhaps you will prefer another girl."

To a servant, Old Capulet gave a paper, saying, "Go throughout Verona and invite to my party tonight the people whose names are written on this paper. Tell them that I look forward to seeing them."

To Paris, Old Capulet said, "Come with me."

Old Capulet and Paris left the room, and the servant said, "Find the people whose names are written here! How can I do that? I can't read! I have been told that the fisherman should use his pencil, and I have been told that the painter should use his net. I think that's what I've been told, but it doesn't sound quite right. But how can I use this piece of paper when I can't read! I must find an educated person."

Old Capulet had hired extra servants for the feast and dance, and so he did not know that this servant could not read.

The illiterate servant walked out into the street and saw Romeo and Benvolio. He did not recognize them, but they looked as if they could read and so he said, "Just the people I need!"

Benvolio said to Romeo, "To put out one fire, firefighters sometimes start another fire. Seeing the pain of another person sometimes lessens one's own pain. One evil is sometimes conquered by another evil. Your eyes have been poisoned by the woman you love; to cure that poison, infect your eyes with the poison of the sight of another beautiful woman."

"Why not simply use aloe vera?" Romeo asked.

"Use aloe vera for what?" Benvolio asked.

"For skinned knees."

"But I'm not talking about skinned knees!"

"You certainly aren't talking about anything I am interested in listening to. Your kinds of remedies have nothing to do with my lovesickness."

Romeo saw the servant eagerly looking at him and asked, "May I help you?"

The servant asked, "Can you read?"

"I can read my own future — I will continue to be miserable."

"That's not the kind of reading I mean, sir. Can you read something that is written on a piece of paper?"

"Yes, if what is written is a language that I can read."

"You are not giving me a strictly straight answer, so I will assume that you do not want to help me," the servant said, beginning to turn away.

"Wait. Don't go. I have been joking with you. I really can read."

The servant handed Romeo the piece of paper and Romeo read the list out loud:

"Signor Martino and his wife and daughters.

"Count Anselm and his beauteous sisters.

"The lady widow of Vitruvio.

"Signor Placentio and his lovely nieces.

"Mercutio and his brother Valentine.

"My uncle Capulet, and his wife and daughters.

"My fair niece Rosaline.

"Livia.

"Signor Valentio and his cousin Tybalt.

"Lucio and the lively Helena."

Romeo said to the servant, "This is a list of well-known people in the city. Mercutio is a friend of mine, and I have seen Rosaline. What is the list for, if you don't mind my asking?"

"They are coming up."

"Up where."

"To my master's house, for supper."

"Whose house?"

"My master's."

"I had hoped for more information than that. Apparently, I was not clear enough when I asked my question."

"I have been joking with you," the servant said. "Now I will tell you what you want to know. My master is the great and rich Old Capulet, and if you and your friend are not Montagues, feel free to crash the party and drink some wine. Farewell, and God bless."

The servant left to invite to the party all the people named in the list.

Romeo and Benvolio had been talking, and Romeo had confessed that the woman he loved was Rosaline, whose name appeared on the list of guests to be invited to the Capulet party.

Benvolio said, "The beautiful Rosaline, whom you say you love, will be at the Capulet party. So will many beautiful women of Verona. Go to the party with me, and if you look with unbiased eyes and compare Rosaline's face with some faces that I shall show you, I will make you think that your swan whom you think is beautiful is actually as ugly as a crow."

"My eyes worship Rosaline, and if ever my eyes would falsely regard any woman as being more beautiful than she, then let my tears turn into fires," Romeo said. "My eyes have often drowned in tears and yet they live, but if ever my eyes regard any woman as being more beautiful than Rosaline, then they are clearly heretics and liars and so should be burnt. Can anyone be fairer than Rosaline? No. Since the creation of the world, the Sun, which sees all, has seen none more beautiful than she."

"Come on," Benvolio said. "When you saw Rosaline and decided that she was beautiful, she was the only woman present. Your eyes had no one to compare her to. Come to the party and compare Rosaline with some women I shall show you, and you won't think Rosaline is as beautiful as you think she is now."

"I will go to the party with you," Romeo said, "but not to look at any women you seek to show me. I will go to the party so that I can look at Rosaline."

In a room in Old Capulet's mansion, Mrs. Capulet and the Nurse were sitting and talking.

"Nurse, where's my daughter? Call her to come to me."

"By my virginity when I was only twelve years old," the Nurse said, "I swear that I have already told her to come here."

The Nurse called, "Lamb! Ladybird!"

Then she said to herself, "Good Heavens! Where is that girl?"

She called again, "Juliet!"

Juliet entered the room and said to the Nurse, "Here I am. What do you want?"

"Your mother wants to talk to you," the Nurse said.

"Here I am, Mother. What do you want?"

"We need to talk about something important," Mrs. Capulet said. "Nurse, step outside for a while. No, wait. Stay here. You should hear what I have to say. You know that Juliet is growing up."

"I can tell her age unto an hour," the Nurse said.

"She still is not yet fourteen years old," Mrs. Capulet said.

"I would stake as a wager fourteen of my teeth — but to my sorrow, I have only four teeth left — that she is not yet fourteen," the Nurse said. "How long is it now to Lammas-tide — the first of August?"

"A fortnight and odd days," Mrs. Capulet replied.

"Even or odd, of all days in the year, on Lammas-eve at night Juliet will be fourteen years old," the Nurse said. "My daughter — God bless Susan's soul — and Juliet were born on the same day. Susan is with God. She was too good for me. But on Lammas-eve at night Juliet shall be fourteen years old. I remember her infancy and childhood well. It has been eleven years since the earthquake and so eleven years since she was weaned. I was her wet-nurse and fed her Susan's milk, and on the day of the earthquake I put wormwood on my nipple to make it bitter. You and your husband were then away visiting the city of Mantua. I was sitting with Juliet in the Sun under the dove-house wall. My memory is excellent. Juliet started to suck at my breast, but when she discovered that the nipple was bitter, she grew irritable. That is when the earthquake struck and the dove-house shook. That is the day that my duties as Juliet's wet-nurse ended. That was eleven years ago, and Juliet was able to stand by herself. Actually, she was able to run and walk by herself, too. The day before the earthquake, she was running and fell forward and cut her forehead. My husband — God bless his soul — said to her, 'Juliet, you fell forward upon your face, didn't you? But someday, after you reach puberty, you will fall backward and lie on your back, won't you, Juliet?' And I swear that pretty Juliet stopped crying and said, 'Yes, I will.'"

Mrs. Capulet blushed, knowing that the joke was that Juliet would lie on her back with her knees in the air and her legs parted — and Juliet would not be alone.

The Nurse continued, "It was the funniest thing. If I live to be a thousand years old, I will not forget it. 'Won't you fall backward, Juliet?' my husband asked her. And pretty Juliet stopped crying and said, 'Yes, I will.'"

"No more of this talk," Mrs. Capulet said. "Please be quiet."

"Yes, I will be quiet," the Nurse said. "But I cannot stop myself from laughing. Pretty Juliet stopped crying and said, 'Yes, I will fall backward,' although she had a bump on her forehead from the fall — a bump as big as one of the balls of a rooster. Juliet fell, and she cried, and my husband said to her, 'You fell forward upon your face, didn't you, Juliet? But one day you will fall backward and lie on your back, won't you, Juliet?' and Juliet stopped crying and said, 'Yes.'"

Juliet was embarrassed because her mother was present, but if her mother had not been present, she would have laughed.

Juliet said, "Please stop telling that story, Nurse."

Having told it four times, the Nurse said, "I am done telling the story. You were the prettiest baby I ever nursed, and I hope that I live long enough to see you married."

"That is exactly what I want to talk about," Mrs. Capulet said. "Juliet, what do you think about getting married?"

Juliet replied, "It is an honor that I have never dreamed about."

"An honor," the Nurse said. She thought, *Yes, if Juliet gets married, her husband will be on her.*

The Nurse said out loud, "That is a wise remark. I would say that you sucked wisdom from my nipples, but that would be complimenting myself as well as you."

Mrs. Capulet said to Juliet, "Think about marriage now. Here in Verona, many ladies of esteem younger than you are already mothers. I myself was a mother when I was your age. Let me tell you straight out that the valiant Paris wishes to marry you."

The Nurse said, "Paris really is a man, Juliet, and such a man! His figure is as perfect as if he were a sculpture."

"Speaking poetically," Mrs. Capulet said, "summertime in Verona has not such a flower as Paris."

"True," the Nurse said, "Paris is a flower."

"What do you say, Juliet?" Mrs. Capulet asked. "Do you think you can love Paris? He will attend our party tonight. Look him over carefully. I think you will be pleased by what you see. If he were a book, a pen of beauty would have written it. Examine his features and see how they work together to create a harmonious whole — he is a handsome man. Continue your examination by looking into his eyes. He will make a handsome groom — he lacks only a beautiful bride. A man needs a woman to be complete. He has handsomeness outside and virtues inside, and with you as his wife, he will be complete. As the wife of such a man, you shall share all his virtues and his reputation. Speaking poetically, by having him as your husband, you will make yourself no less."

The Nurse joked, "Juliet, you will certainly be no less. Women grow by men — they become pregnant!"

"Tell me, Juliet," Mrs. Capulet said. "Can you learn to return Paris' love?"

"I will look at him and see if I like him," Juliet said. "I certainly will not do anything that you do not want me to do."

A servant entered the room and said to Mrs. Capulet, "The guests have arrived and dinner is supposed to be ready. People are asking for you and for Juliet. Servants in the pantry are cursing the Nurse because she is not there to help. Everything is a mess right now, and I have to go back and serve the food. I beg you, come with me and restore order."

"We will go with you," Mrs. Capulet said.

She said to Juliet, "Paris is here now, and he wants you to approve of him as a groom."

The Nurse said, "Juliet, seek happy nights to happy days. A honeymoon has many happy nights."

On a street of Verona, Romeo, Mercutio, Benvolio, and five or six other people wearing masks and some people holding torches to provide light were heading to Old Capulet's party. Mercutio was neither a Montague nor a Capulet, but he was a friend to Romeo and Benvolio and other Montagues. He was also related to Prince Escalus.

"When we arrive at the party, should we talk to Old Capulet and introduce ourselves, or should we simply crash the party?" Romeo asked.

"We need not say anything," Benvolio said. "Wordy introductions are out of fashion. We need not draw attention to ourselves. We certainly aren't going to blindfold one of ourselves like Cupid, arm him with a bow, and scare all the ladies like a scarecrow scares crows. We don't need such ostentatious costumes, and we don't need any memorized complimentary speeches. We will simply crash the party anonymously and let them judge us as they will. We will dance a dance, and then we will be gone."

"Let me hold a torch," Romeo said. "I am not in the mood for dancing."

"No, good friend Romeo," Mercutio said. "We must watch you dance."

"You would not enjoy the sight," Romeo replied. "You, Mercutio, have dancing shoes with nimble soles. I have a soul of lead that weighs me down so I cannot dance."

"You are a lover," Mercutio said. "You can easily borrow Cupid's wings. With them you can dance lighter than a non-lover."

"Not so," Romeo said. "I am so wounded by Cupid's arrow that I cannot soar with his light feathers. Because I am so wounded, I cannot leap in a dance. Under love's heavy burden, I sink."

"By sinking, you drag down love," Mercutio said. "Love is so tender that it ought not to be treated like that."

"Is love tender?" Romeo asked. "Love treats me roughly, rudely, and boisterously, and it pricks like a thorn."

"If love is rough with you, then you should be rough with love," Mercutio, who regarded sex as a joke, said. "If love pricks you, then use your prick to lay down your love and be satisfied."

They had arrived at Old Capulet's mansion. Mercutio shouted, "Someone, give me a mask to put my face in. Give me a new face for my old face. And make the new face ugly. What do I care if people look at me and think that my face is deformed?"

Someone handed Mercutio an ugly mask. He looked at it and said, "Here are the overhanging beetle brows that shall make me look deformed!"

Benvolio said, "Let's knock and go in. As soon as we are in, let all of us begin dancing."

"Give me a torch to hold," Romeo said. "Let people who are light of heart do the dancing. If I hold a torch and am an onlooker only, I probably won't get in trouble. I am not in the mood for dancing, and so I won't dance. I am done with dancing."

"Done with dancing?" Mercutio said. "Dun is the color of a mouse, and now we should be quiet like a mouse. We should stop talking and go in to the party and start dancing. If you are dull-colored and dun, we will pick you up out of the mire caused by your lovesickness — that mire in which you are up to your ears. Come on, we need to go in to the party. We are wasting light."

"No, we aren't. It's night," Romeo said.

"Please," Mercutio said. "We are wasting the light cast by our torches by not going in to the brightly lit party. It is like lighting a lamp on a bright summer day when the lamp is not needed. Don't think so literally. Usually, you are a wit."

"We mean well by going to this party," Romeo said, "but we are not showing wit or intelligence by so going."

"Why not?" Mercutio asked.

"I dreamt a dream tonight."

"And so did I."

"What was your dream?"

"That dreamers often lie."

"In bed asleep, while they do dream about true things," Romeo, who could be witty, said.

Mercutio, as was common with him, let his imagination run free: "Oh, then, I see Queen Mab has been with you. She is the fairies' midwife, and she is no bigger than the agate-stone on a ring on the forefinger of an alderman. She rides in a wagon drawn by a team of tiny insects across men's noses as they sleep. The spokes of the wheels of her wagon are made from spiders' long legs. Covering her wagon are the wings of grasshoppers. The traces used by the insects to draw her wagon are made from the webs of spiders. The collars that go around the necks of the insects are made of moonbeams. Her whip handle is made from a cricket's bone, and the lash of her whip is made from a fine filament. Her wagoner is a small grey-coated gnat that is not as big as a round little worm touched by the lazy finger of a maiden. Her chariot is the shell of a hazelnut, and it was manufactured by a carpenter squirrel or an old grub, which for ages have made the coaches of fairies."

Mercutio's vision gradually grew darker: "And in this carriage Queen Mab gallops night by night through the brains of lovers, and then they dream of love. She gallops over the knees of courtiers, and then they dream of curtsies. She gallops over the fingers of lawyers, and then they dream of lawyers' fees. She gallops night by night over the lips of ladies, who dream of kisses. Queen Mab blisters those lips because they smell of candy. Sometimes she gallops over the nose of a courtier, and then he dreams of smelling out a lawsuit. Sometimes she takes the tail of a tithe-pig — a gift to support a priest — and she uses it to tickle the nose of a parson, and then he dreams of money and wealth."

And then Mercutio's vision became very dark: "And in this carriage Queen Mab sometimes drives over the neck of a soldier, and then he dreams of cutting foreign throats, of breaking through defensive walls, of ambushes, of Spanish swords, and of drunkenness. She drums in his ear and he wakes up. Frightened, he prays and makes vows to God, and then he goes back to sleep. She is that very Queen Mab who makes matted the manes of horses in the night, and tangles their hairs in foul elflocks that, once untangled, are harbingers of misfortune. Queen Mab is the hag who sends dreams that teach maidens to lie on their backs and screw and get pregnant and carry children like women of good carriage. Queen Mab is she who —"

Alarmed by Mercutio's wildness, Romeo touched him gently on the arm and said, "Peace, peace, Mercutio, peace! Be quiet now. You are talking of nothing."

As if he were coming out of a trance, Mercutio blinked himself into everyday consciousness and said, "True, I talk of dreams, which are the children of an idle brain and are born of nothing but vain fantasy that is as thin of substance as the air and that is more unconstant than the wind, which now blows toward the frozen bosom of the north, but then becomes angry and blows toward the dew-dropping south."

"We are being blown off our course by the wind you talk of," Benvolio said. "We are supposed to be attending a party. By now, everyone has eaten. Soon, people will start leaving the party and going home."

Romeo thought, *Benvolio worries about getting to the party too late. I worry about getting there too early. I worry that an uncaring fate and the uncaring stars will set something in motion at this party that shall end with my all-too-early death. But let who or whatever has the steerage of my course direct my sail!*

Romeo said out loud, "Let's go party-crashing, friends!"

Benvolio said to a drummer, "Begin drumming," and all marched into the mansion of Old Capulet.

Inside Old Capulet's mansion, musicians played. Some servants were busy cleaning up the great chamber after the dinner.

A servant asked, "Where's Potpan? Why isn't he helping us to carry dirty dishes away from the table? How can he call himself a server? He isn't scraping any dishes and washing them!"

A second servant said, "When almost everyone forgets to do their work, and it lies in the hands of only a couple of workers to do all the work, then it is a foul thing — and the good workers' hands are foul with the work of scraping dirty plates."

The first servant said, "Let's carry out of the dining room the folding chairs and movable cupboard and the silver dishes and the silverware. Please, save me a piece of marchpane — I love sugar and almonds. And please, tell the porter to let in Susan Grindstone and Nell. Our master is having a party, and we have a party of our own planned."

The first servant then called, "Anthony and Potpan!"

Anthony and Potpan arrived.

Anthony asked, "What do you want?"

"Help is needed in the great chamber," the first server said. "They have been asking for your help for a long time."

Potpan said, "We cannot be here and there, too. Be cheerful, boys; work hard and quickly, and then we will have time for our party."

In the great chamber, Old Capulet invited guests and maskers to dance. Juliet was nearby.

Wearing masks and not easily recognized, Romeo and his friends entered the great chamber.

Old Capulet said, "Welcome, gentlemen! Ladies who are not plagued with painful corns on their feet will be happy to dance with you. Ladies, none of you will dare not to dance, now! Any lady who does not dance will — I will tell everybody — have corns on her feet. Welcome, gentlemen! I have seen the day when I have worn a mask and would whisper sweet nothings in a fair lady's ear, but for me those days are gone. You are welcome, gentlemen! Musicians, play! Clear the hall. Dance, everyone! Foot it, girls!"

Mercutio, Benvolio, and others in Romeo's group began to dance. Romeo stood to the side like a wallflower.

Old Capulet ordered, "More light, you knaves. Move the tables to the side. Quench the fire because the room has grown too hot."

Old Capulet, who had not recognized Romeo, said to a relative about Romeo and his group of friends, "I had not expected these people in masks to be guests, but the more the merrier — especially welcome are those who will dance. You and I are past our dancing days — how many years has it been since you and I wore a mask at a party?"

His relative answered, "By Saint Mary, it must be thirty years."

"What?" Old Capulet said. "It can't have been that long ago! We last wore a mask at the wedding of Lucentio at Pentecost. When Pentecost arrives, it will have been twenty-five years since Lucentio was married."

"He has been married longer than that. His son is thirty years old."

"That's not possible, is it?" Old Capulet said. "Just two years ago, his son was still a minor."

Romeo had caught sight of Juliet, and her beauty dazzled him. He asked a servant, "Which lady is she who is dancing with that knight?"

The servant replied, "I don't know, sir." Old Capulet had hired extra servants for the feast and dance; these servants were not familiar with the Capulet household.

Still wearing a mask, Romeo thought, *She teaches the torches how to burn brightly. She seems to brightly hang upon the cheek of night like a rich jewel in an Ethiopian woman's ear. Her beauty is too rich for use and too dear for Earth! She is like a white dove in the midst of a flock of black crows — that is how much in beauty she surpasses all the other women in this ballroom. Once this dance is finished, I will watch where she stands, and I will touch her hand and make blessed my own rough hand.*

Then Romeo said out loud without thinking, "Did my heart ever love before now? Answer no, sight! For I never saw true beauty until this night."

Although Romeo thought that he was speaking softly, Tybalt overheard him enough to recognize the sound of his voice but not enough to understand the content of his words.

Tybalt said to a servant, "This person, judging by his voice, is a Montague. Fetch me my rapier, boy. How does this slave dare to come hither, his face covered with a grotesque mask, to mock and scorn our dance? By the stock and honor of my kin, to strike Romeo dead, I hold it not a sin."

Old Capulet noticed that Tybalt was upset, and he asked him, "What's wrong? Why are you so angry?"

Tybalt replied, "Uncle, this man is a Montague, our enemy. He is a villain who has come here in spite, to mock our dance this night."

Old Capulet looked closely at the young man whom Tybalt pointed out, and he asked, "Young Romeo, is it?"

Tybalt replied, "Yes, he is that villain Romeo."

Mindful that the Prince of Verona had threatened him with death should violence break out, Old Capulet said, "Don't be angry, Tybalt. Let him alone. He bears himself like a good gentleman, and to say the truth, he has a reputation throughout Verona of being a virtuous and well-behaved youth. I would not for the wealth of all Verona have any harm come to him in my house. Therefore, Tybalt, be patient and take no note of him. Instead, I want you to show a fair presence. Look pleasant, be courteous, and don't frown. Remember that you are at a dance."

"My frowns are justified, when a guest is such a villain," Tybalt said. "I will not endure Romeo's presence."

A younger man should not disrespect an older man, especially when the older man is a wealthy and respected relative and the host of a dance that the young man is attending.

Old Capulet told Tybalt, scornfully, "I say that you shall endure Romeo's presence here. You will do what I tell you to do, young man! Who is the master here? Me? Or you? Who are you to make a scene? No one, that's who!"

"But, uncle, it's a shame!"

"Says you!" Old Capulet replied. "Are you going to disrespect me? Do so, and your actions will come back and bite you in the ass. Don't be a fool."

He said to some nearby guests, "Enjoy yourselves and be merry!"

He then said to Tybalt, "You are acting like a spoiled youngster! If you can't behave, leave before you make a fool of yourself."

He said to some servants, "More light, more light!"

He then said to Tybalt, who looked ready to burst with words, "Be quiet, or I'll make you quiet."

He said to some guests, "Be merry, friends."

Tybalt, still angry, thought, *Patience and anger don't mix. I am so angry that I cannot be patient, and so I shall leave. Romeo's intrusion here must seem to him sweet, but I shall change the sweetness to bitter gall.*

Tybalt left the great chamber.

Juliet had stopped dancing, and Romeo — whose name means "a pilgrim to Rome" — went over to her and held her hand, saying, "If I profane with my unworthiest hand this holy shrine, your hand, the gentle fine is this: My lips, two blushing pilgrims, ready stand to smooth that rough touch with a tender kiss."

Juliet, using the same metaphor of a pilgrim — sometimes also called palmers — visiting a holy shrine, replied, "Good pilgrim, you do wrong your hand too much. By holding my hand, you show proper devotion. For saints have hands that pilgrims' hands do touch, and palm-to-palm is holy palmers' kiss. By holding my hand, you have showed proper devotion, but let's not otherwise kiss."

Romeo asked, "Have not saints lips, and holy palmers, too?"

"Yes, pilgrim," Juliet said. "They have lips that they must use in prayer."

"Oh, then, dear saint, let our lips do what our hands are doing — let our lips touch. My lips pray to you for a kiss. Grant their prayer, lest my faith turn to despair."

"Saints do not take the initiative, even when through the intercession of God they grant prayers."

"Then move not, while you grant my prayer. Thus from my lips, by yours, my sin you take."

Romeo kissed Juliet.

"Now my lips have the sin that they have taken from your lips," Juliet said.

"Your lips have taken sin from my lips?" Romeo said. "That is a trespass I sweetly urged! Give me my sin again."

He kissed her again.

Juliet said, "You kiss by the book — you get your kisses in accordance with the pilgrim metaphor we have been following."

The Nurse arrived and said to Juliet, "Madam, your mother craves a word with you."

Juliet left, and Romeo asked the Nurse, "Who is her mother?"

The Nurse replied, "Young man, her mother is the lady of the house, and a good lady, both wise and virtuous. I was wet nurse to her daughter, with whom you have been talking. Whoever marries her will inherit much wealth from her father."

The Nurse went to Juliet.

Romeo thought, *She is the only daughter of Old Capulet! My life is forfeited to my enemy! If I can't be with Juliet, I cannot live!*

Benvolio came over to Romeo and said, "It is time for us to leave — we have had a good time here."

"Yes," Romeo said. "I wonder if I ever again will have as good a time."

Old Capulet heard the two talking and said, "No, gentlemen, don't leave now. Stay and eat a snack before you go."

Benvolio shook his head no, and Old Capulet said, "What? You must leave? Then I thank you gentlemen for coming tonight. Good night, young sirs."

Old Capulet said, "Bring more torches here to provide light for these gentlemen."

Romeo and Benvolio waited for Mercutio to come, and Old Capulet said to Juliet and the Nurse, "It really is getting late, so I'm going to bed."

Old Capulet left, but Juliet and the Nurse stayed.

Juliet still did not know the name of the young man who had kissed her, and she did not want the Nurse to know that she was interested in him, so she asked what were the names of some other young men before she asked for the name of the young man who had kissed her.

Juliet pointed and asked the Nurse, "Who is that gentleman?"

The Nurse replied, "The son and heir of old Tiberio."

"Who is that person who is now going out of the door?"

"He, I think, is young Petruchio."

Juliet pointed and asked, "Who is the young man who would not dance?"

"I don't know."

"Please go and ask him his name."

The Nurse left to inquire, and Juliet thought, *If he is married, I think that I will die. My grave will be my wedding bed.*

The Nurse returned and said, "His name is Romeo, and he is a Montague. He is the only son of your great enemy."

Juliet said softly, "My only love sprung from my only hate! I saw and loved him before I knew who he was, and I found out who he is too late to stop loving him. Love is born in me, and I now love a loathed enemy."

"What did you say?" the Nurse asked.

"Just a rhyme that I learned at this dance."

Someone in another room called, "Juliet."

The Nurse said loudly, "We're coming! We're coming!"

She said to Juliet, "Let's go now. The guests have all left. All who remain are family and servants."

They left.

CHAPTER 2: ROMEO AND JULIET BECOME ENGAGED

Prologue

Romeo's old "love" for Rosaline has now died, replaced by Romeo's new love for Juliet. Romeo had suffered during his "love" for Rosaline and he had thought that he would die, but Rosaline's beauty could not compare with the beauty of Juliet. Juliet now loves Romeo, and Romeo loves Juliet. But Romeo must tell a Capulet — his enemy — that he loves her. Juliet also loves her enemy. Because Romeo is a Montague male, he has little opportunity to meet Juliet again and tell her of his love. Because Juliet is a Capulet female, she has even less opportunity to meet Romeo and tell him of her love. But they are passionately in love, and love will find a way, a time, and a place, and the danger they place themselves in when they meet will be sweetened with extreme pleasure.

Running, Romeo appeared in a lane by the wall of Old Capulet's garden. He wanted to be alone and he wanted to see Juliet, and so he was running away from Benvolio and Mercutio.

Romeo said to himself, "How can I leave this lane when Juliet is so near? Let my body stay here and seek my soul, whose name is Juliet."

Romeo climbed the wall and jumped down into Old Capulet's garden.

Benvolio and Mercutio arrived in the lane by the wall of Old Capulet's orchard. They were seeking Romeo.

Benvolio called, "Romeo! Where are you, Romeo?"

Mercutio said, "Romeo is wise, and I swear on my life that he has gone home to his bed."

Benvolio disagreed: "He ran this way, and he climbed this garden wall. Call him, good Mercutio."

"I will call him, and I will entreat him to reveal himself," Mercutio replied. "Romeo! Romantic man! Madman! Passionate man! Lover! I conjure you to speak to us with a sigh. Speak but one rhyme, and I will be satisfied that you are well and did not break your neck and die when you jumped down from the wall. Sigh 'Ah, me!' Say 'love" and 'dove.' Speak a word to Venus, goddess of love. Speak the name of her son Cupid, who shoots his arrows as if love were blind, as when he made King Cophetua fall in love with a beggar-maiden and make her his Queen."

Mercutio said to Benvolio, "Romeo does not hear me. He does not stir. He does not move. The poor fool is dead, and I must conjure him alive!"

Mercutio called, "I conjure thee by Rosaline's bright eyes, by her high forehead and her scarlet lip, by her fine foot, straight leg, and quivering thigh, and by the foxhole that there adjacent lies, that you appear to us!"

"If he hears what you are saying about Rosaline, he will be angry," Benvolio said.

"What I say cannot anger him," Mercutio said. "If I wanted to anger him, I would conjure up a male spirit to put some maleness in her honeyhole, leaving it there arisen until she laid it and conjured it down. That would make him angry. Benvolio, you are a good man, and you want me to speak of a conjurer's circle, but I know of better, wetter circles to speak about. What I am saying now, however, is fair and honest. The purpose of my conjuration is merely to say the name of the woman Romeo loves and thereby make him rise — at least a part of him."

"Romeo has hidden himself among these trees," Benvolio said. "He wants the night to be his company. Love is blind, and so Romeo seeks the night."

"If love is blind, how can a lover's arrow hit the target's circle?" Mercutio asked Benvolio. "Romeo will now sit under a tree and wish that his beloved lass were the medlar fruit that young ladies call 'open-ass' when they think that young men are not around to overhear them. I wish that Romeo were a pear — a pear that from the right angle looks like a standing-up penis and balls. In fact, I wish that Romeo were a poperin pear. With an open-ass lass and his pop-er-in pear, Romeo would be able to put his dick in her butt."

Benvolio looked shocked.

Mercutio then called, "Romeo, good night! I'm going home to my warm bed. It's too cold for me to sleep out in the open."

He said to Benvolio, "Shall we go?"

"Let's go," Benvolio replied. "It's useless to seek someone who does not want to be found."

— 2.2 —

In Old Capulet's garden, Romeo listened to Benvolio and Mercutio leave.

Romeo said about Mercutio, "He who jests at the scars of love has never felt a wound."

Juliet appeared at a window on the second story above Romeo.

Romeo said softly, "What light through yonder window breaks? The window is the East, and Juliet is the Sun. Arise, fair Sun, and kill the envious Moon, who is already sick and pale with grief because you are far more beautiful than she. Diana, the Moon, is a virgin goddess, and you, Juliet, serve her because you are still a virgin. Diana is envious of you. Don't serve the Moon — the vestal clothing of her and her followers is sick and green, and only fools wear it. Cast off Diana's vestal clothing — stop being a virgin!

"Here is Juliet! Here is my love! I wish that she knew I love her! She speaks yet she says nothing out loud, but so what? Her eyes speak. I will answer her eyes. But I assume too much — she is not speaking to me.

"Two of the brightest stars in all the Heavens, about to leave on business, beg her eyes to twinkle in their spheres until they return. What if her eyes were in the Heavens, and the two stars were in her head? The brightness of her cheeks would shame those stars, as daylight shames a lamp. Her eyes in Heaven would through the airy region stream so brightly that birds would sing and think it were not night. See, how Juliet leans her cheek upon her hand! Oh, that I were a glove upon her hand, that I might touch her cheek!"

Juliet said, "Sorrow defines my life."

Romeo said to himself, "She speaks out loud. Speak again, bright angel! You are as glorious to me this night, standing in a window over my head, as is an angel — a winged messenger of Heaven — to the upturned wondering eyes of mortals who fall back to gaze on him when he bestrides the lazy-pacing clouds and sails upon the bosom of the air."

Still not knowing that Romeo was in the garden beneath her window, Juliet said, "Romeo, Romeo! Why is your name Romeo? Deny your father and refuse your name — stop being a Montague. Or, if you will not do so, swear that you love me, and I will no longer be a Capulet."

Romeo said to himself, "Shall I hear more, or shall I speak to Juliet?"

Juliet said, "Only your name is my enemy. If you give up your name, you will still be yourself. What is the name Montague? It is not hand, or foot, or arm, or face, or any other part belonging to a man."

Juliet paused to smile at "part belonging to a man," then she continued, "Be some other name! What's in a name? That which we call a rose by any other name would smell as sweet. If Romeo were not named Romeo, he would still be perfect. Romeo, put aside your name. In the place of your name, which is not part of you, take all of me."

Romeo said out loud to Juliet, "I take you at your word — I believe what you have said. Call me your love, and I'll be baptized a second time and take a new name. Henceforth, my name will not be Romeo."

Not immediately recognizing Romeo's voice, Juliet said, "Which man are you who, hidden by the night, have heard what I have said?"

Romeo replied, "I have a name that I don't know how to tell you because, dear saint, my name is hateful to myself because it is an enemy to you. If my name were written down, I would tear up my name."

Juliet said, "My ears have not yet heard a hundred words of your tongue's utterance, yet I know by the sound of your voice who you are. Aren't you Romeo and a Montague?"

"I am neither, dear saint, if you dislike them."

"How did you come here, and why?" Juliet asked. "The garden walls are high and hard to climb, and for you this place is death because you are a Montague. If any of my relatives find you here, they will kill you."

"With love's light wings did I fly over these walls," Romeo said. "Stony walls cannot stop love and keep love out. Whatever love can do, that will love attempt. Your relatives cannot stop me or my love for you."

"If my relatives see you, they will murder you."

"An angry look from you would hurt me more than twenty of their swords," Romeo said. "But if you look at me sweetly, their hatred cannot hurt me."

"I would not for the world have them see you here."

"The night will hide me," Romeo said. "But if you do not love me, let them find me here. It is better for them to kill me than for me to go on living without your love."

"How did you find this place?"

"Love caused me to make inquiries and find it," Romeo said. "Love lent me wisdom, and I lent love eyes. I am no pilot; yet, if you were as far away as that vast shore washed with the farthest sea, I would risk taking the journey there for such a prize as you."

"Because of the darkness of the night, you cannot see my face, but if you could see my face, you would see a blush because of the words you have overheard me speak," Juliet said. "I could put on an act and deny what I said, but I won't do that. Let me ask you straight out: Do you love me? I know that you will say 'Yes,' and I know that I will believe you. Still, even if you swear that you love me, you may be lying. They say that Jove, the Roman king of the gods, laughs at the perjuries of male lovers. Romeo, if you really do love me, tell me the truth. But if you think that I am won too easily, I will play hard to get, if that will make you woo me, but I prefer not to play games. To be honest, fair Montague, I love you too much, and you may think me too easy, but trust me, gentleman, and I will be true to you, unlike those girls who only pretend to be virtuous. I should not have revealed my love for you so quickly, I admit, but you overheard my confession before I was aware that you were present. Therefore, pardon me. Do not think that because I have confessed so quickly during this dark night that I am not serious."

Romeo started to reply romantically and poetically, "Lady, I swear by the blessed Moon that tips with silver all these fruit-tree tops —"

"Do not swear by the Moon, the inconstant Moon, that monthly changes in her circled orbit. If you swear by the ever-changing Moon, perhaps your love for me will change into a love for someone else."

"What shall I swear by?"

"Do not swear at all, or if you must swear, swear by your gracious self, for you are the god of my idolatry. If you do so, I will believe you."

"If my heart's dear love —"

"Do not swear," Juliet said, changing her mind. "You bring me joy, but I have no joy of our contact tonight. It is too rash, too unadvised, too sudden. It is too much like the lightning, which ceases to be before one can say 'It lightens.' My sweet one, good night! This bud of love, ripening by the breath of summer, may prove a beauteous flower when next we meet. Good night, good night! May you enjoy the same sweet repose and rest that I feel within my breast!"

"Will you leave me so unsatisfied?"

"What satisfaction can you have tonight?"

"The exchange of your love's faithful vow for mine."

If Romeo had been a different kind of man — a man such as Mercutio — he would have asked for a different kind of satisfaction.

"I gave you my vow of love before you asked for it," Juliet said. "I wish that I could take back that vow of love."

"Why would you want to take it back?" Romeo asked.

"So that I could once more tell you for the first time that I love you," Juliet replied. "But really, I am wishing for something that I already have: for you and me to be in love. My love for you is as boundless as the sea. My love for you is as deep as the sea. The more love I give to you, the more love I have left to give because my love for you is infinite."

The Nurse called from within the mansion, "Juliet!"

Juliet said to Romeo, "I hear some noise within. Dear love, goodbye!"

She shouted to the Nurse inside the mansion, "Just a minute!"

Then she said to Romeo, "Sweet Montague, be true. Stay but a little while, and I will come to the window again."

Juliet went inside to talk to the Nurse, and Romeo said to himself, "Blessed, blessed night! I am afraid lest that, this being night, all this is only a dream. It seems too flattering-sweet to be real."

Juliet reappeared at the window and said, "Three words, dear Romeo, and good night indeed."

In this society, people would say that they wanted to speak "a word" more when they had more to say. Juliet's three words are, no doubt, "I love you."

Juliet continued, "If your love for me is honorable and you want to marry me, send me a message tomorrow by a person whom I will send to you. In your message tell me where and at what time you will marry me, and all my fortunes at your foot I will lay and I will follow you, my husband, throughout the world."

The Nurse called from within, "Juliet!"

Juliet called to the Nurse, "I'm coming!"

Juliet then said to Romeo, "But if your love for me is not honorable, I beg you —"

The Nurse called, "Juliet!"

"Just a minute!" Juliet called, and then she said to Romeo, "But if your love for me is not honorable, I beg you to stop wooing me and to leave me to my grief. Tomorrow I will send someone to you."

Romeo began, "So thrive my soul —"

But Juliet said, "A thousand times good night!" and went inside.

Romeo complained to himself, "Being away from you is a thousand times worse than being close to you. A lover goes toward his lover as eagerly as a schoolboy goes away from his books. A lover goes away from his lover as sorrowfully as a schoolboy walks to school."

He began to leave, but Juliet reappeared at the window.

Not seeing Romeo, she hissed, "Romeo!" She was trying to be loud enough to be heard by Romeo but not so loud as to be heard by her family and the Nurse.

Juliet said, "I wish I could shout as loudly as a falconer who calls his falcon back to him. That way, Romeo would hear me. But I cannot shout. I must be hoarse and not draw my family's attention, or I would make use of the voice of Echo, who was so talkative that Juno, Queen of the gods, punished her by making her repeat the words of other people. I would shout 'Romeo' into the cave where Echo lives, and she would repeat his name. Her voice would say his name so many times that it would grow more hoarse than mine."

Romeo heard Juliet, and he returned to her.

He said, "Juliet, who is my soul, calls my name: How silver-sweet sound the tongues of lovers by night! They are like the softest music to attentive ears!"

"Romeo!" Juliet called.

"Yes, Juliet?"

"At what time tomorrow shall I send a messenger to you?"

"Nine in the morning."

"I will not fail. It will seem like twenty years until nine a.m. comes."

She turned to go inside, then turned back, hesitated, and said, "I have forgotten what else I wanted to say to you."

"Let me stand here until you remember it."

"I shall forget on purpose in order to have you still stand there because I love to be with you."

"And I will continue to stay here, and let you continue to forget. I will forget that I have any other home than right here."

"It is almost morning. Because of the danger you would face if you were found here, I would have you go, and yet I want you to go no further than a spoiled child's bird. The child lets the bird hop a small distance from her hand like a poor prisoner in his twisted chains, and with a silk thread pulls it back to her. The child does not want the bird to leave her."

"I wish that I were your bird."

"So do I," Juliet said. "But if I act like that now, I will get you killed by keeping you here too long. Good night! Good night! Parting is such sweet sorrow, that I shall say 'good night' until it be tomorrow."

She departed.

Romeo said to himself, "May sleep dwell upon your eyes, and may peace be in your breast! I wish that I were sleep and peace, so I could be with you. Now I will go to my priest's home to beg for his help and to tell him about my good fortune."

Friar Lawrence was up early and was out in a meadow collecting herbs and placing them in his wicker basket. He talked to himself as he looked at the plants around him, "The morning smiles at the frowning night. As the morning brightens the Eastern sky, the night like a drunkard staggers away from the light and the Sun. Before the Sun is fully risen and has made the day cheerful and has dried up the dew of the night, I must fill my basket with poisonous weeds and with medicinal flowers. The Earth is the mother of nature, but it is also her tomb. The place for burial is also her womb. And from the Earth's womb come so many and various children that we can make use of. Many plants have many excellent qualities, no plant lacks a use, and all of the plants are different. Herbs, plants, and seeds all have useful qualities. None is so evil but that its use can bring about good, and none is so good but that, being misused, it can bring about evil. Virtue itself can become a vice, if it is used wrongly, and vice can bring into being something good when used to good purpose."

Romeo walked toward the good friar, who did not see him and continued to talk to himself, "In this small flower are both a poison and a medicine. Smell this flower, and you will feel good and your senses will tingle. Taste this flower, and your senses will die along with your heart. In plants, as well as in human beings, two kings attempt to rule. One king is good and full of grace, and the other king is evil and filled with an evil will. When evil becomes predominant, a cankerworm will feed on the leaves of that plant and kill it."

Romeo said, "Good morning, Friar Lawrence."

Friar Lawrence looked up and said, "*Benedicte*! God bless you! Who is up so early? Ah, it is Romeo. Young man, you must have a troubled mind if you are up and out of bed so early. Old men have troubles and cares, and sleep does not come easily to or remain long with men who worry, but a young man who is unbruised by life and who has an untroubled mind should easily go to sleep and easily stay asleep. Since you are up so early, something must be worrying you. Or if nothing is worrying you, I can guess why you are now up — our Romeo has not been in bed and asleep tonight."

"Your second guess is correct," Romeo said. "I have not been in bed and asleep tonight, but for all that, the sweeter rest was mine."

Shocked by what entered his mind, Friar Lawrence said, "God pardon sin! Have you been up all night with Rosaline?"

"With Rosaline, Friar Lawrence?" Romeo said, "No. I have forgotten that name, and the sorrow that name brought me."

"Good for you, my son," Friar Lawrence said. "But then where have you been?"

"I'll tell you, before you ask me again. I have been feasting with my enemies. One of my enemies wounded me, and I wounded her. To cure our wounds, we need your help and a holy sacrament. I bear no hatred, blessed man, because what I ask you will benefit my enemy."

"Be plain, good son, and let me understand your speech; riddling confession finds but riddling absolution."

"Then plainly know that my heart's dear love is set on Juliet, the beautiful daughter of rich Old Capulet. My heart is set on her, and her heart is set on me. We have been wounded by love and separated by our families, and the only thing that will cure our wounds is marriage, for then we can come together. When and where and how Juliet and I wooed each other and exchanged vows of love, I will tell you, but this I pray, that you will consent to marry us today."

"Holy Saint Francis, what a change is here!" Friar Lawrence said. "Is Rosaline, whom you did love so dear, so soon forsaken by you? Young men's love then lies not truly in their hearts, but in their eyes. Jesu Maria, what a deal of brine used to wash your love-sickened cheeks for Rosaline! Your tears seasoned your love for Rosaline with salt, but you did not taste that love! The Sun has not yet cleared away the mist from your lovesick sighs for Rosaline! Your lovesick groans for Rosaline ring yet in my old ears. Here upon your cheek I see a still-unwashed stain of a tear that you shed for Rosaline! If ever you were yourself and these woes were yours, you belonged to Rosaline and your woes were all for her! And now you have changed? Remember this: Don't blame women for falling in and out of love, when men do the same."

"Often you have criticized me for loving Rosaline," Romeo said.

"I criticized you for your puppy love, not for any real love, Romeo."

"And you wanted me to bury my love."

"I did not want you to bury your love in a grave just so you could immediately love someone else."

"Please, don't criticize me," Romeo said. "The woman whom I now love returns my love. Rosaline did not love me."

"She knew well that you talked of love without understanding what love is. You were like a student who has memorized the answers to questions without understanding what the answers mean. But come with me, changeable lover, I will help you because a marriage between you and Juliet will most likely change the hatred between the Montagues and the Capulets into love."

"Let's hurry," Romeo said. "I want to be married quickly."

"Go wisely and slow," Friar Lawrence said. "People who run fast stumble."

Benvolio and Mercutio walked together on a street.

"Where the devil is Romeo?" Mercutio said. "Did he go home last night?"

"He did not return to his father's mansion," Benvolio replied. "I asked his servant there about him."

"That same pale hard-hearted wench, that Rosaline, is tormenting him, and so he will surely become insane."

"Tybalt, that Capulet, sent a letter to Romeo's father's mansion."

"It is a challenge to a duel, I suppose," Mercutio said.

"Romeo will answer him," Benvolio said.

"Any man who can write may answer a letter."

"He will not answer it with another letter. Instead, he will fight Tybalt, just as Tybalt dares him to do."

"Poor Romeo!" Mercutio said. "He does not need a duel to kill him. He is already dead. The dark eyes of the white wench Rosaline have already stabbed him. A love song has already shot him through the ear. The center of his heart has already been penetrated by Cupid's arrow. Is Romeo, an already dead man, the man who should fight Tybalt?"

"Why shouldn't he fight Tybalt?" Benvolio asked.

"Romeo is too love struck to fight anyone, including Tybalt, who is as intelligent as the cat — also named Tybalt — that Reynard the Fox tricks in folk tales. Tybalt is quite the man. In fact, Tybalt likes to think that he is a manly man with manly man powers. Tybalt speaks well in public — truly, Tybalt is a courageous captain of compliments. Tybalt fences the way that other people sing classical music — Tybalt and they keep time, distance, and proportion. They reach a high note, and Tybalt puts his sword in your bosom — with his sword Tybalt can stab and butcher each button on your chest. Tybalt understands the protocol and the moves of fencing: the first and second cause, the immortal *passado*, the *punto reverso*, and the home thrust!"

"I don't understand those words," Benvolio said.

"If you knew how to fence and duel the fashionable way, you would," Mercutio replied. "But those words are too fancy! The people such as Tybalt who use them are inane, lisping, drama-queen fanatics! They pronounce these fancy words with fake accents! They say, 'By Jesu, he is a very good blade! He is a very brave man! She is a very good whore!' It is lamentable that we should be thus afflicted with people like Tybalt — these strange buzzing insects, these fashionmongers, these pretentious fellows with their elaborate courtesy, who pay so much attention to fashionable clothing and language that they cannot sit at ease upon an old bench! I am tired of people such as Tybalt forever saying '*Bon! Bon!*' when all they mean is 'Good! Good!' Romeo may be too lovesick to fight Tybalt, but I could easily defeat Tybalt in a fair fight."

Romeo came walking up to his friends.

Benvolio said, "Here comes Romeo."

"Romeo is thin," Mercutio said. "His lack of a lady who loves him in return has made him grieve in love-sickness and waste away. He is like a herring that has separated from its roe and dried. Take 'roe' away from 'Romeo' and you have 'meo' — a lover's sigh. Now the grieving lover is ready to listen to the love poetry of Petrarch. Compared to Rosaline, Laura — the beloved of Petrarch — was only a kitchen-wench. Compared to Rosaline, Dido — the tragic Queen of Carthage who loved the Trojan hero Aeneas, who abandoned her — was a dowdy woman. Compared to Rosaline, Cleopatra — the Queen of Egypt — was a gypsy. Compared to Rosaline, Helen of Troy and the woman named Hero — loved respectively by Paris and by Leander — were good-for-nothing harlots. Compared to Rosaline, the pretty eyes of Thisbe, the lover of Pyramus, were lacking. So Romeo thinks, anyway."

Mercutio said to Romeo, "Signor Romeo, *bon jour*! There's a French salutation to go with the French loose breeches you are wearing. You gave us the counterfeit last night."

"Good morning to both of you," Romeo said. "What counterfeit did I give you?"

"You counterfeited friendship with us — and then you gave us the slip and disappeared, although we sought you," Mercutio said.

"Pardon me, my friend Mercutio," Romeo said. "I had something important to do, and in such circumstances, I ought to be excused for my lack of good manners."

"I can guess that your important business involved going in and out and in and out," Mercutio said.

"Going in and out of doors?" Romeo said.

"That's not what I meant, but your interpretation of my words is very polite. I was referring to a kind of exercise."

"I am in the pink of health," Romeo said.

"In the pink is exactly what I was referring to," Mercutio said.

"Knowing you, 'pink' has more than one meaning, and not just one sole meaning," Romeo said.

"Knowing you, you are concerned about your soul," Mercutio said.

"At times, my soul is my sole concern, and I'm not talking about the sole of my shoes, or the Sun, or King Solomon," Romeo said.

"Benvolio, help me out," Mercutio said. "I am running out of puns. I can't think of any more to save my soul."

"If you can't make any more puns, then I declare myself the winner in this game of wits," Romeo said. "I am a cobbler of puns. I will save your sole and I will heel you, but I will not dye — D, Y, E — for you."

"Shoe puns are shoe hilarious," Mercutio said. "Trying to find a new pun at this point is like going on a wild-goose chase. Some of these puns are hoary with age."

"I have never seen you go out of your way to avoid a whore," Romeo said.

"I will bite you on the ear for that joke," Mercutio said.

"Whores use their mouths on a different body part," Romeo said. "Which is why their customers say, 'Please don't bite.'"

"Your wit is a sharp sauce that betters the living of life. You are a *bon vivant*," Mercutio said.

"You have always liked a saucy girl — someone who betters the living of life. You are also a *bon vivant*," Romeo said.

"Your wit runs both broad and deep."

"You like broads and you like being deep in the pink."

"Isn't this game of punning much better than being constantly lovesick and groaning?" Mercutio said. "You are again the Romeo I remember. You are friendly. You are good company. You are witty. You are what you used to be and what we have wished you to be. For a while, the love you felt made you run up and down like an idiot with his tongue or another body part hanging out while he looked for a hole to put his favorite plaything in."

"That is a good place to stop this line of thought," Benvolio said.

"But I like this line of thought," Mercutio said.

"You like going too far and too fast," Benvolio said.

"You are wrong," Mercutio said. "I like going very deep and very fast."

The Nurse and Peter, another Capulet servant, entered the street.

"Here comes some fun," Romeo said.

It was a windy day, and the wind blew on and filled out the Nurse's long skirt and Peter's baggy shirt.

"A sail, a sail!" Romeo shouted.

"No, two sails," Mercutio said. "A shirt and a smock."

The Nurse said, "Peter."

"Yes, Nurse."

"Please give me my fan."

"Good Peter, give her fan so that she can hide her face," Mercutio said under his breath to Romeo and Benvolio. "Her fan is fairer than her face."

The Nurse said, "Good morning, gentlemen."

Mercutio replied, "Good afternoon, fair gentlewoman."

"Is it afternoon?" the Nurse asked.

"Indeed, it is," Mercutio said. "The bawdy — that is, dirty — hand of the dial is now on the prick — that is, mark on a clock — of noon. Prick, hand, ha! Handjob! A prick in two hands is not worth one in a bush."

"Your language is bawdy," the Nurse said. "What kind of man are you?"

Romeo said, "He is a man whom God created so that he could ruin himself."

"He is well on his way to doing that," the Nurse said.

She added, "Gentlemen, can any of you tell me where I may find the young Romeo?"

"I can tell you," Romeo said, "but young Romeo will be older when you have found him than he was when you sought him. However, in Verona I am the youngest of that name, for fault of a worse."

"You speak well," the Nurse said.

"True," Mercutio said to Benvolio, "'For fault of a worse' is a nice variation of 'for want of a better.'"

"If you are Romeo," the Nurse said to Romeo, "I wish to speak to you and have a confidence with you."

"She means 'conference,' not 'confidence,'" Benvolio whispered to Mercutio. "She will probably 'endite,' not 'invite,' him to supper."

"I have found out her occupation," Mercutio said.

"What have you found out?" Benvolio asked.

"She is a procurer. She can't be a whore because she is so old and ugly. Of course, she may be a hoary hairy whore who wants to serve him a hair pie. Would you like to hear a song that I learned at school?"

He sang loudly as he stared at the Nurse,

"She has a friend with some hankers.

"He has crabs, herpes, syphilis, and cankers.

"He got all the four

"From a dirty old whore,

"So he wrote her a letter to thank her.'"

The Nurse stared in shock as Mercutio then said, "Romeo, are you going to your father's for lunch? We will go with you."

"You two go now, and I will follow you later," Romeo replied.

Mercutio tipped his hat to the Nurse with mock courtesy and said to her, "Farewell, ancient lady, farewell."

Then he and Benvolio walked away as Mercutio sang again, "She has a friend with some hankers ...."

Recovering from her shock, the Nurse asked Romeo, "Who was that sassy punk whose mouth runs faster than his mind?"

"He is a gentleman who loves to hear himself talk," Romeo said. "He says more in words in one minute than he says in sense in a whole month."

The Nurse said, "If he says anything nasty about me, I will take him down, and if he is bigger than anything I can handle, I will find other people to take him down. Either I or other people whom I will find will demolish him. We will indeed make him go down in size and make him shorter than he is now."

Romeo thought, *It is a good thing that Mercutio is not here. He would make jokes about going down and about demolishing a six-inch structure.*

"He is a scurvy knave!" the Nurse continued. "I am not one of his loose women. I am not one of his gangster's molls. I am not one of his buddies."

She said to Peter, "And all you did was stand by and let him use me as the butt of his jokes. Now everyone will know that he used me."

"I saw no one use you," Peter said. "If I had, I would have quickly taken my weapon out."

Romeo thought, *I am glad that Mercutio is not here to talk about a weapon. The weapon that Mercutio would talk about is one that a man can take out of his pants. And, of course, he would make jokes about this woman being used.*

Peter continued, "I dare draw a sword as soon as another man, if I see occasion in a good quarrel, and if the law is on my side."

Romeo thought, *Once again, I am glad that Mercutio is not here to talk about a sword. He would talk about a "swordsman," a word that can refer to a guy who has had a lot of sex. He would joke about putting a sword in a sheath. He would remind everyone that the Latin word "vagina" means sheath.*

"I swear to God that I am so angry that every part about me quivers," the Nurse complained.

Romeo thought, *If Mercutio were here, he would make a joke about an arrow in a quiver.*

The Nurse continued, "That scurvy knave! But to business. Romeo, my young lady ordered me to find you. I am her Nurse. What she told me to say to you, I will keep to myself for now. First, I want to tell you that if you are trying to mislead her into a fool's paradise — that is, if you want a one-night stand instead of a marriage — that is a poor way to treat a lady. My young lady is very young, and even if she were not, no lady should be treated that way."

"Nurse," Romeo said. "Tell Juliet that my intentions are honorable. I —"

"I will do so," the Nurse said. "Lord, she will be a joyful woman."

"What will you tell her, Nurse?" Romeo asked. "You have not listened to what I have to say."

"I will tell her, sir, that you do protest to her," the Nurse said. "That is what a gentleman would do."

Protest to her? Romeo thought. *Oh, she means, Propose to her.*

Romeo said, "Tell her to find an excuse to go to Friar Lawrence's cell this afternoon. There she and I shall be married."

He held out some money to the Nurse and said, "This is for your pains."

The Nurse said, "No, truly, sir; not a penny."

"I insist that you take it," Romeo said.

The Nurse took the money, and then she said, "This afternoon, you say. Juliet will be there."

"Wait, good Nurse, behind the abbey wall," Romeo said. "Within an hour my servant shall be here with a rope ladder. I will use it to climb into Juliet's bedchamber tonight and be with her joyfully and secretly. Farewell. Do good work and I'll reward you. Farewell. Be sure to praise me when you speak to Juliet."

"May God bless you," the Nurse said, "but listen to me."

"What is it?"

"Can your servant keep a secret?" the Nurse asked. "Let us remember that two people can keep a secret provided that only one person knows the secret."

"My servant can keep a secret," Romeo said. "He is as true as tempered steel."

"My young lady is the sweetest lady," the Nurse said. "I remember when she was a babbling little girl and fell forward upon her face — but no more of that. A nobleman in town — Count Paris — would gladly marry Juliet and bed her, but Juliet prefers to look at a toad, a very toad, than look at him. I made her angry by saying that Paris is better looking than you. When I told her that, she changed color."

The Nurse paused, then said, "Don't rosemary and Romeo both begin with the same letter?"

"Yes," Romeo said. "They both begin with R."

"Don't be silly. Pirates say, 'Arrrrr.' So do sea dogs. I know of a dog that when it talks, it says, 'Arrrrr.' Perhaps that is its name. Are you mocking me because I'm not educated? I'm pretty sure that Romeo and rosemary begin with another letter. Anyway, Juliet says the most beautiful things about you and rosemary."

Romeo said, "Please say the most beautiful things about me to Juliet."

"Yes, I will," the Nurse said. "I will say one thousand nice things about you."

Romeo left, and the Nurse called, "Peter!"

Peter, who was standing a short distance away, said, "Yes, Nurse?"

The Nurse ordered, "Peter, take my fan, and walk in front of me. Walk quickly."

In Old Capulet's garden, Juliet impatiently waited for the Nurse.

Juliet said to herself, "The clock struck nine when I sent the Nurse to see Romeo. She promised to return in half an hour. Maybe she could not find and talk to him — I doubt that. She must be lame because she returns home so slowly. People who carry the messages of lovers should be as fast as thought, which is ten times faster than the beams of the Sun that drive back shadows from dark hills in the morning and make the hills brightly lit. Swift-winged doves carry messages from Venus, goddess of love, and the wings of Cupid are as swift as the wind. Now the Sun is at high noon, and it is three long hours that the Nurse has been away and still she has not returned. If she were young and had the passions of youth, she would be as swift in motion as a ball. My words would send her as quickly as a sharply hit tennis ball to Romeo, and his words would return her to me just as quickly. But old folks behave as if they were already dead — they are as unwieldy, slow, heavy, and pale as lead."

Catching sight of the Nurse, Juliet said, "Here she comes!"

The Nurse and Peter entered Old Capulet's garden, and Juliet said, "Oh, honey nurse, what news do you bring me? Did you meet him? Send Peter away."

The Nurse told Peter, "Wait at the gate."

Juliet said, "Now, good sweet nurse — why do you look so sad? Even if the news you bring me is sad, yet tell it merrily. If the news is good, you are perjuring it with your sour face."

"I am tired," the Nurse said. "Let me rest awhile. My bones ache. I had to search everywhere to find Romeo."

"If I could, I would give you my bones, provided that you gave me your news. Speak, good Nurse. Tell me your news."

"Why are you in such a hurry?" the Nurse said. "Can't you wait a minute? Can't you see that I am out of breath?

Juliet said, "How can you say that you are out of breath when you have breath to tell me that you are out of breath! The number of words you say to persuade me to wait are many more than the number of words it would take you to tell me what I want to know. Is your news for me good or bad? Tell me!

Tell me either good or bad right now, and I will wait a while for the details. Tell me! Is your news good or bad?"

"You made a foolish choice when you chose Romeo as a good-looking beau," the Nurse said. "But he is more handsome than other men, his legs are more handsome than other men's, as are his hands and feet and his body. Ladies ought not to talk like this about a man, but yes, Romeo is truly handsome in face and body. Romeo is not the flower of courtesy — he can be rude. But I swear that he is as gentle as a lamb. Do whatever you want, Juliet. But always obey God."

The Nurse paused, then added, "Have you eaten lunch yet?"

"No, I haven't eaten yet," Juliet said. "But you are not telling me what I want to know — I already know that Romeo is handsome. I want to know whether he and I will be married. What did he tell you about that?"

"I have a headache," the Nurse said. "My head is pounding as if it will break into twenty pieces. And my back — ow!"

Juliet began to rub one side of the Nurse's back; the Nurse said, "The other side. You should be ashamed for sending me out to run all over Verona — I could die from exhaustion!"

"Truly, Nurse," Juliet said. "I am sorry that you are not well, but sweet, sweet, sweet nurse, tell me, what did Romeo tell you?"

"Romeo, your love, says, like an honest gentleman, and a courteous gentleman, and a kind gentleman, and a handsome gentleman, and, I believe, a virtuous gentleman, he says —"

Then, forgetting what she was about to say, and starting to think about something else, the Nurse asked, "Where is your mother?"

"Where is my mother!" Juliet said. "Why, she is inside. Where else should she be? How oddly you answer my questions! You tell me, 'Romeo, your love says, like an honest gentleman, Where is your mother?'"

"Why are you so angry?" the Nurse said. "Is this how you treat my aching bones! From now on, deliver your own messages!"

"I have no time to argue with you," Juliet said. "Tell me! What did Romeo tell you?"

"Do you have permission to go to confession today?"

"Yes, I have."

"Then go to Friar Lawrence's cell. You will find there a groom who wants to make you his wife."

Juliet blushed.

"The Nurse said, "Now comes the red blood up in your cheeks. Now that you are in love with Romeo, you blush at any news concerning him. You go to church now. I will take a different path. I need to be given a rope ladder that Romeo will use to climb up to your bedchamber as soon as it is dark. Right now, I am doing all the work. But tonight — when Romeo comes — you shall do the work of a woman. Go now. I will eat lunch. You go to Friar Lawrence's cell."

"Wish me luck," Juliet said. "Honest nurse, farewell."

Romeo was waiting for Juliet in Friar Lawrence's cell.

Friar Lawrence said, "May the Heavens smile upon this holy act of the marriage sacrament so that we shall not regret it later."

"Amen," Romeo said, "but even if sorrow comes later, it shall not equal the joy I feel when I look at Juliet for just one short minute. Join our hands in holy matrimony, and then love-devouring Death can do whatever he wishes — it is enough for me that I can call Juliet mine."

"Be careful, Romeo," Friar Lawrence said. "These violent delights have violent ends, and in their triumph they die. They are like fire and gunpowder, which as they kiss, they explode. Honey in moderation is delicious and sweet, but too much honey can make you hate its taste. Therefore, love moderately if you wish love to last long. Too fast can harm love as much as too slow."

Friar Lawrence looked outside and said, "Here comes your lady. Her foot is so light that the flint of the rocky road of life will not cut it. A lover is so light that he or she can walk on a string that was spun by a spider and is floating in the air and not fall off. Lovers are light, and so is the love of lovers."

Juliet arrived at Friar Lawrence's cell. She immediately ran to and hugged Romeo tightly. They did not let go of each other.

"Good afternoon, Friar Lawrence," Juliet said.

Romeo kissed Juliet.

"Romeo greets you for both of us," Friar Lawrence said.

Juliet said, "I return his greeting," and she kissed Romeo.

"Juliet," Romeo said, "if your joy is as much as mine, then use your skill with words, which is greater than mine, to fill the air with sweet words and rich verbal music and tell me how happy our marriage will be."

Juliet replied, "True understanding of happiness focuses on being happy and not on talking about happiness. Experiencing happiness is better than talking about happiness. Beggars can use words to count what they have. The wealth of love I give and the wealth of love I receive is so great that I cannot count even half of my wealth of love."

"Come with me now," Friar Lawrence said. "We will have the wedding quickly. I can see by the way you kiss and hug and speak to each other that I had better not leave you alone until after I have married you. Not until after you are married shall you two become one."

He led the happy couple away to be married.

CHAPTER 3: ROMEO AND JULIET ENJOY THEIR WEDDING NIGHT

— 3.1 —

Mercutio, Benvolio, and some others were in a public square on a very hot and sticky day — a muggy day that made everyone irritable.

Benvolio said, "Mercutio, let's go home. The day is hot, the Capulets are out and about, and, if we meet, we will fight each other. Today is so hot that everyone is a bad mood and ready to fight."

Mercutio, always ready to make a joke, decided to treat Benvolio, a peacemaker, as if he were a troublemaker.

Mercutio replied, "You are like one of those fellows who when he enters a tavern puts his sword upon the table and says, 'I hope to God that I will not need you,' but after his second drink draws his sword and wants to fight — without provocation — the person who drew his drink."

Benvolio asked, "Am I like such a fellow?"

"Don't try to deny it," Mercutio said. "When you are in the mood to fight, you are as quick to get in a fight as any man in Italy. You are so quick-tempered that when you want to get in a fight, you quickly find something to make your temper rise."

"Is that so?"

"If there were two such men as you, very quickly there would be but one left, because one man would kill the other," Mercutio said. "You will start a fight with a man because he has a hair hair more or a hair less in his beard than you do. You will start a fight with a man who is cracking nuts. Why? Because your eyes are the color of hazelnuts. Only your eyes would spy such a quarrel. Your head is as full of quarrels as an egg is full of protein, and because of excessive fighting your head is as scrambled as an egg. You fought a man because he coughed in the street and woke up your dog that was lying in the sunshine. You fought a tailor because he wore a new jacket before Easter. You fought a different tailor because he tied his new shoes with old shoelaces. And yet you are acting like a man who wishes to keep me from fighting!"

"If I were as likely as you to quarrel," Benvolio said, "my future life expectancy would be about 15 minutes."

"Don't be silly," Mercutio said.

"Look," Benvolio said. "Some Capulets are coming our way."

"I don't care," Mercutio replied.

Tybalt and some other Capulets walked up to Mercutio and Benvolio.

Tybalt said to the other Capulets, "Stay close to me. I will speak to them."

Tybalt was like a schoolyard bully who wanted protectors close to him.

He said to Mercutio and Benvolio, "Gentlemen, good afternoon. I would like to have a word with you."

"Just one word?" Mercutio asked, widely parting his legs. "That's not enough. Make it a word and a blow."

Tybalt, who thought that Mercutio was speaking about fighting, said, "You shall find me apt enough to do that, sir, if you give me enough reason."

"Aren't you capable of finding enough reason without me giving you a reason?"

"Mercutio, you band together with Romeo," Tybalt said.

"Band together?" Mercutio said. "Do you think that we are musicians? If you think that, you will listen to nothing but noise."

Mercutio touched his sword and said, "Here is my fiddlestick. It can make you dance. Band! Indeed!"

Benvolio said, "We are out here in public. Either we should go somewhere private and talk together rationally, or we should all leave and go home. Out here in public everyone can witness what we say and do."

"Men's eyes were made to look, so let them look," Mercutio said. "I will not leave this place."

Romeo entered the public square and walked toward the group of people.

Tybalt said, "Well, peace be with you, sir. Here comes the man I want to see."

"He is a man, but not your man," Mercutio said. "But if you want him to be your follower, walk to a dueling ground. He will follow you, and he will fight you."

Tybalt said, "Romeo, the hatred I have for you makes me call you by no better word than this — you are a villain."

These were fighting words, and Tybalt — and everyone else present, including Mercutio and Benvolio — expected Romeo to fight Tybalt.

He did not.

Romeo, newly married to Juliet and therefore an in-law to Tybalt, replied in a friendly way, "Tybalt, I have reason to treat you well — indeed, even love you. Because of that reason, which you don't now know about, I decline to take offence at your insult to me. I am not a villain. Therefore, farewell. You really do not know who I am."

Romeo turned away from Tybalt, who drew his sword and said, "Boy, your words shall not excuse the insults that you have made to me; therefore, turn and draw your sword."

Romeo replied, "I say that I have never harmed you, but I do love you better than you can know. Soon you shall know the reason of my love. And so, good Capulet — you bear a name I love as dearly as my own — do not be angry and do not attempt to fight me."

Mercutio, shocked by Romeo's words, shouted, "This is calm, dishonorable, vile submission! A mere threat makes Romeo submit!"

Mercutio said to Tybalt, "Tybalt, you rat-catcher, will you walk away from me?"

"What do you want?"

Mercutio drew his sword and said, "Tybalt, you king of cats, I want nothing but one of your nine lives. I will take one, and depending on how you act, I may very well beat the rest of your eight lives out of you. Will you pluck your sword with its hilts, which look like ears, out of your scabbard? Be quick about it, or you will find my sword moving about your ears before you draw your sword!"

"If you want to duel, I am the man for you," Tybalt replied, drawing his sword.

"Mercutio, please put away your sword," Benvolio said.

"You may begin your attack," Mercutio said to Tybalt.

They started to fight.

Romeo put himself between the two duelists and said, "Draw your sword, Benvolio, and beat down their weapons. Gentlemen, stop this outrage! Tybalt, Mercutio, you know that Prince Escalus has forbidden fighting in the streets of Verona! Stop, Tybalt! Stop, Mercutio!"

Tybalt thrust his sword under Romeo's arm and mortally wounded Mercutio. Seeing Mercutio wounded, Tybalt and the other Capulets ran away.

Most fights among teenagers involve bluster, not blood. Sometimes, a fight goes wrong and someone gets hurt.

Mercutio said, "I am hurt! May a plague curse all the Capulets and all the Montagues! I've been wounded! Has Tybalt gone, and suffered nothing? Did no one fight for me?"

Disbelieving, Benvolio said, "What! Have you been wounded?"

"Yes, I have suffered a scratch," Mercutio said. "It will do. Get me a doctor."

"Your wound cannot be serious," Romeo said.

"No, it is not serious. It is not as deep as a well or as wide as a church door, but it will do — it will serve as well as a serious wound."

Mercutio knew that he was dying, and he knew exactly what to do — make a pun, the best pun of his short life. He told Romeo, "Ask for me tomorrow, and you shall find me a *grave* man."

He added, "I have suffered my deathblow. I am done for this world. What is a dog, a rat, a mouse, a cat doing scratching a man to death? Tybalt is all of these, as well as a braggart, a rogue, and a villain who fights by a rulebook. He is not a man who should be able to kill me."

Mercutio said to Romeo, "Why the devil did you come between us? Tybalt thrust his sword under your arm and mortally wounded me."

"I thought I was doing the right thing," Romeo said.

Mercutio said, "Help me into some house, Benvolio, or I shall faint. May the plague infect all the Capulets and all the Montagues! The Capulets and the Montagues have made me food for worms! I am done for! A plague! On both families!"

Benvolio carried Mercutio away.

Romeo said to himself, "Mercutio, a gentleman and Prince Escalus' near relative, my best friend, was mortally wounded fighting for me because Tybalt stained my reputation with his slander — Tybalt, who has been my in-law for an hour! Sweet Juliet, your beauty has made me effeminate and has taken away my bravery, softening the steel that used to be my valor!"

Benvolio returned and said, "Romeo, Mercutio is dead! His gallant soul has climbed past the clouds, scorning too quickly this world he leaves behind."

"This day's black fate will not end today," Romeo said. "Black fate will rule other days. On this day begins great sorrow, and many days will pass before the sorrow ends."

Benvolio looked up and said, "Tybalt is coming back to the scene of his crime."

Tybalt and his followers did not know how badly Mercutio was wounded, but they wanted to know. If Mercutio were badly wounded or dead, Tybalt needed to go into hiding until he could flee from Verona and save his life.

"Tybalt is still alive while Mercutio is dead!" Romeo said. "Not for long. Mercy, leave me and return to Heaven — I have no need of you! All I need now is fire-eyed fury!"

Tybalt faced Romeo.

Romeo said, "Now, Tybalt, take back the insult you gave me earlier. I am no villain. The late Mercutio's soul has not gone far. It is only a little way above our heads, waiting for your soul to join it and keep it company. Either your soul, or my soul, or both, must leave this world and accompany Mercutio's soul."

"You were Mercutio's friend while he was alive," Tybalt said. "It is fitting that your soul accompany his soul in its journey."

"Our fight will determine whose soul accompanies his soul."

Romeo and Tybalt fought with swords, and Romeo killed Tybalt so quickly that Benvolio did not have time to intervene to stop them. As Mercutio had known, Tybalt ably talked the talk but he could not ably walk the walk. Mercutio had died because of Tybalt's lucky thrust with a sword made while Romeo was trying to part the two fighters.

Benvolio said, "Romeo, run away! I hear people and guards coming! You have killed Tybalt, and Prince Escalus has decreed that anyone who fights in the streets of Verona shall die! If the guards catch you, the Prince will order you to be killed! Run away! Now!"

"Oh, I am fortune's fool!" Romeo cried. "I am the plaything of fate."

Benvolio shouted at him, "Why are you still here!"

Romeo ran for his life.

Some guards and citizens arrived and asked Benvolio, "Where is the man who killed Mercutio, Prince Escalus' relative? Which way did he run? Where is Tybalt, the murderer?"

If Romeo had restrained himself and had not killed Tybalt, Prince Escalus would have had Tybalt arrested and punished — perhaps with death.

Benvolio said, "Tybalt lies here, dead."

A guard told Benvolio, "You are under arrest, in the name of Prince Escalus. Come with me."

Prince Escalus arrived, as did Old Montague and Old Capulet, their wives, and other people. Prince Escalus asked, "Where are the vile people who have disturbed the peace of our city?"

"Prince Escalus," Benvolio said, "I can tell you everything that happened. Here lies the body of Tybalt, who killed Mercutio, your relative. Romeo killed Tybalt."

Grieving, Mrs. Capulet said, "Tybalt was my nephew! He was my brother's child! And now he is dead. Prince, I demand justice. Tybalt's blood has been spilled. For blood of ours, shed the blood of Romeo Montague."

Prince Escalus wanted justice — his own relative, Mercutio, had been killed — and he wanted peace in his city, but he also wanted to find out exactly what had happened.

He asked, "Benvolio, who began this bloody fight?"

Benvolio replied, "Tybalt lies here dead, slain by Romeo, but Romeo spoke peacefully to Tybalt, asking him to think about how trivial was the cause of Tybalt's anger at him. He also urged him to remember your order against fighting in the streets. Romeo said all this with gentle breath, calm look, and his knees humbly bowed, but Tybalt was not willing to be peaceful. Tybalt pointed his piercing steel at the breast of Mercutio, who was as angry as Tybalt and whose sword met Tybalt's sword. Mercutio, scorning Tybalt, beat aside Tybalt's deadly thrusts with his sword and sent deadly thrusts back at Tybalt, who beat them aside. Romeo cried aloud, 'Stop, friends! Stop fighting!' He then used his arm to beat down their swords. Tybalt thrust his sword under Romeo's arm and mortally wounded Mercutio, and then Tybalt fled. Soon, he came back, and Romeo, angered at the death of Mercutio, sought revenge, and the two fought like lightning, and before I could part them, haughty Tybalt lay dead. Romeo then fled. This is the truth; if it is not, order me to be killed."

Mrs. Capulet said, "Benvolio is a Montague, and he is lying to protect another Montague. Some twenty Montagues fought in this black strife, and all those twenty could kill only one life: that of Tybalt. I beg for justice, which you, Prince Escalus, must give. Romeo slew Tybalt, and so Romeo must not live."

Prince Escalus replied, "Romeo slew Tybalt, but Tybalt slew Mercutio. How many more shall die?"

"Not Romeo, Prince Escalus," Old Montague said. "He was Mercutio's friend. Romeo's fighting ended what the law should have ended: the life of Tybalt."

Prince Escalus made up his mind: "And for that offence immediately we do exile Romeo from Verona. I have been affected by the feud between the Montagues and the Capulets: Mercutio, my kinsman, is dead. I will punish both families with so heavy a fine that you shall all repent the death of Mercutio. I will be deaf to pleading and excuses; neither tears nor prayers shall persuade me to let you off lightly. Don't even try it. Romeo must leave this city quickly. If he is found here after this day, the hour that he is found will be his last hour alive. Take this corpse away, and obey my orders. Pardoning murderers is not merciful because it leads to more murders."

In her bedchamber, Juliet impatiently waited for night to come so that Romeo could come to her.

Juliet said to herself, "Phaëthon went to his father, the god Apollo, and asked to be allowed to drive the Sun-chariot across the sky and bring light to the world. But Phaëthon, doomed youth, was unable to control the stallions, and they ran wildly away with the Sun-chariot, wreaking havoc and destruction upon Humankind and the world. The king of the gods, Jupiter, saved Humankind and the world by throwing a thunderbolt at Phaëthon and killing him.

"Right now, you stallions that pull the Sun-chariot, I want you to race the Sun across the sky to the West and sunset so that Romeo may quickly come to me. Gallop as if Phaëthon were once again your charioteer and make it dark night immediately. Close the curtain upon day, so that the stallions may sleep and Romeo may leap into my arms with no one to see him and raise an alarm. Lovers by the light of their own beauty can see enough to have sex in the dark, or, if love be blind, it best agrees with night. Come, night, clothed in black, and teach me to lose my virginity to Romeo, my husband.

"Night, cover the blood — the blood of a virgin — that rises in my cheeks until I experience sex for the first time and know that sex with a true love is right and proper. Come, night. Come, Romeo. Cum, Romeo, who is day in night. In my vision of you, I see your white body lying upon the black wings of night — you are whiter than new snow on the back of a raven.

"Night, give me my Romeo, and when he cums and 'dies' with delight, take him and cut him out in little stars. If you do that, he will make the face of the nightly Heaven so fine that all the world will be in love with night and pay no worship to the garish Sun."

Having expressed her strong desire to lose her virginity quickly to Romeo, her husband, Juliet said, "Romeo and I belong to each other, but neither of us has so far done anything that shows it. It is as if I have bought a mansion but have not moved into it. Romeo has married me, but he has not yet enjoyed me. My waiting now for Romeo to come to me is like an impatient child's waiting during the eve before some festival at which the child will wear new clothing."

Juliet saw the Nurse coming to her and said, "My Nurse is bringing me news. Anyone who says 'Romeo' speaks with Heavenly eloquence."

The Nurse, carrying a rope ladder, entered Juliet's bedchamber.

Juliet asked, "Nurse, what news do you have?" Seeing that the Nurse was carrying something, Juliet asked, "What do you have in your hands? Is that the rope ladder that Romeo sent to you?"

The Nurse threw down the rope ladder and replied, "Yes, it is."

Juliet asked, "What is troubling you? What is the news? Why are you wringing your hands?"

The Nurse said, "This is a miserable day. He's dead! He's dead. He's been murdered! We're ruined, Juliet. We're ruined!"

Juliet, assuming that Romeo had died, said, "Can Heaven be so cruel?"

The Nurse said, "Romeo can be that cruel, but Heaven cannot. Oh, Romeo, Romeo! Who ever would have thought it? Romeo!"

"What kind of devil are you, who torments me so?" Juliet said. "This kind of torture belongs in Hell. Has Romeo killed himself? If you say, 'Yes, he has killed himself,' I will die just as surely as if a basilisk had looked at me and struck me dead. If Romeo is dead, say 'yes.' If Romeo is not dead, say 'no.' Those short words will determine whether I live or die."

"I saw the wound, I saw it with my eyes," the Nurse said. "It was on his breast. It was a corpse to be pitied — a bloody corpse to be pitied, Pale, pale as ashes, all red with blood — I fainted at the sight."

"Heart, cease to beat," Juliet said. "Eyes, go to prison and never look on liberty. Dust that makes up my body, return to the dust of the Earth. Life, stop — Romeo and I shall share one grave."

"Oh, Tybalt, Tybalt, the best friend I had!" the Nurse said. "Oh, courteous Tybalt! You were an honest gentleman! That ever I should live to see you dead!"

"What storm is this that blows so contrary?" Juliet said. "From which direction are the squall winds blowing? Is Romeo slaughtered, and is Tybalt dead? Is my dearly loved cousin dead, and also my dearer lord, my husband? Is the trumpet blowing that announces the end of time? Nurse, tell me! Who is living, and who is dead?"

"Tybalt is dead, and Romeo has been banished from Verona," the Nurse replied. "Romeo killed Tybalt, and that is why he is banished."

"Oh, God!" Juliet said. "Did Romeo's hand really shed Tybalt's blood?

"It did! It did!" the Nurse said. "Curse the day, it did!"

"Romeo is not what he seemed to be!" Juliet said. "Oh, serpent heart, hid with a flowering face! Did ever dragon keep so fair a cave? Beautiful tyrant! Angelical fiend! Dove-feathered raven! Wolvish-ravening lamb! Despised substance of divinest show! Romeo is in reality a complete opposite to what he seemed to be. He is a damned saint, an honorable villain! What laws of Nature had to be broken to put the spirit of a fiend from Hell into the sweet fleshly paradise of Romeo's body? Was there ever a book containing such vile matter so beautifully bound? I can't believe that deceit should dwell in such a gorgeous palace!"

"There's no trust, no faith, no honesty in men," the Nurse said. "All men lie and cheat, and all men are evil. Where is the servant? He needs to bring me a drink. These griefs, these woes, these sorrows make me old. Go to Hell, shameful Romeo!"

"Blistered be your tongue for such a wish!" Juliet said. "Romeo was not born to shame; upon his brow shame is ashamed to sit, for Romeo's brow is a throne where honor may be crowned King. I should not have criticized my husband the way I did."

"Will you speak well of the man who killed your cousin?" the Nurse asked.

"Should I speak ill of the man who is my husband?" Juliet asked. "Poor Romeo, who will speak well of you, when I, your wife of three hours, have said such bad things about you? But why, villain, did you kill my cousin? No doubt because that villain cousin would have killed you, my husband. Back, my foolish tears, return back to my eyes, your native spring. Tears belong to sorrow, and I am joyful that my husband lives, whom Tybalt would have killed. I must be joyful that Tybalt is dead because he would have killed my husband. All of this is comforting news, so why am I crying? One thing happened that is worse than Tybalt's death. That thing is expressed in one word that murders me. I wish I could forget that word, but it is burned into my brain like damned guilty deeds are burned into the minds of sinners. Tybalt is dead, and Romeo — banished. That word 'banished' creates more sorrow in me than the deaths of ten thousand Tybalts. Tybalt's death was woe enough; no more sorrow should have been added to that sorrow. But if sour woe delights in company and must be accompanied by other griefs, why was not the death of Tybalt followed by the death of my father or my mother, or both? That would have been bad enough, and I would have grieved in the ordinary way. But following the news of Tybalt's death, I have been ambushed with the news of Romeo's banishment. To hear 'Romeo is banished' is to tear my world and my life apart. It is as if my father, my mother, Tybalt, my husband, and myself were all dead. 'Romeo is banished!' There is no end, no limit, no measure, no bound to the grief that short sentence brings. No words can express that grief."

Juliet then asked, "Where are my father and my mother, nurse?"

"They are weeping and wailing over Tybalt's corpse. Will you go to them? I will lead you there."

"They can use their tears to wash his wounds," Juliet said. "When they have finished crying, I will still be crying because of Romeo's banishment. Take away that rope ladder. Romeo wanted to use it to climb into my bedchamber tonight, but he is exiled from Verona. I, still a virgin, will become a virgin widow. I will go to my wedding-bed alone. The grave — not Romeo — will take my virgin body."

"Go to your bedchamber," the Nurse said. "I will find Romeo so he can comfort you. I know where he is. Listen to me. Romeo will come to you tonight. He is now hiding in Friar Lawrence's cell."

"Find Romeo, and give him — my true knight — this ring," Juliet said. "Have him come to me to take his last farewell."

Entering his cell, Friar Lawrence said loudly, "Come out, fearful Romeo. Figuratively speaking, affliction is in love with you, and you are married to calamity."

Romeo came out from behind a curtain where he had been hiding in case the city guards had come for him, and he said, "Friar Lawrence, what is the news? What is the Prince's ruling about me? What sorrow is in store for me that I am still unaware of?"

"Romeo, you are too much afflicted with suffering. I bring you news of the punishment that Prince Escalus has set for you."

"Is the Prince's sentence upon me anything less than my death?"

"He has given you a gentler punishment than that," Friar Lawrence said. "Your punishment is not your body's death but instead your body's banishment."

"Banishment!" Romeo said, throwing himself upon the floor and lying there in despair. "If you want to be merciful to me, say instead that my punishment is death. To me, exile from Juliet is more terrifying than death. Do not say that I am banished."

"You are banished from Verona," Friar Lawrence said, "Bear this punishment patiently, for the world is broad and wide."

"For me, no world exists outside Verona," Romeo said. "Outside the walls of Verona lie Purgatory and torture — in fact, Hell itself. To be banished from Verona is to be banished from the world — and to be banished from the world is to be dead. Banishment is another, nicer, word for death. By telling me that I am banished, you are cutting off my head with a golden axe, and you are smiling while you make the swing of the ax that kills me."

"You have the wrong attitude," Friar Lawrence said. "You are guilty of the sin of ingratitude. Your lack of appreciation is shocking! The penalty for what you did is death, but merciful Prince Escalus has softened your punishment. He turned the black word 'death' into the merciful word 'banishment.' You have received much mercy, but you don't see or appreciate that."

"Banishment is torture, not mercy," Romeo said. "Heaven is here, where Juliet lives. Every cat and dog and little mouse, every unworthy thing, may live here in Heaven and look at Juliet, but I may not. Even the flies of Verona have it better than I do. They may touch Juliet's hand or her virgin lips, which grow red when they touch each other, thinking such self-kisses a sin. But I cannot touch Juliet's hand or her lips. Flies may do this, but I must fly from Verona and Juliet. Flies are free, but I am banished. And yet you tell me that banishment is not death? Haven't you got a better way to kill me than through banishment? Haven't you got any poison or a sharp knife or some other disgraceful way of killing me? The damned in Hell use the word 'banishment' — they are banished from Heaven and they howl when they say the word 'banishment.' You are a priest to whom I confess my sins. You absolve my sins, and you profess to be my friend. How then can you torment me with the word 'banishment'?"

"You foolish madman, listen to me."

"Why? You will speak again of banishment."

"I can give you armor against that word," Friar Lawrence said. "Philosophy can lessen adversity. Philosophy can comfort you even though you are banished."

"Again you say the word 'banished'! Philosophy is worthless unless it can make a Juliet, or bring Verona — and Juliet! — to my place of exile, or change Prince Escalus' mind about my punishment! Philosophy does not help. Philosophy is unable to provide comfort when I am banished. Talk to me no more."

"I see that madmen have no ears."

"Why would they, when wise men have no eyes?"

"Let me talk to you about the situation you are in."

"You cannot speak about what you cannot feel," Romeo said. "If you were as young as I am, if you loved Juliet the way I do, if you had been married for only an hour when you killed Tybalt, and if you were banished from the one you love, then you could speak, then you could tear your hair, and then you could fall upon the ground as if you were falling into your grave. If all that has happened to me had happened to you, then you would act exactly the way I am acting."

Someone knocked at the door of Friar Lawrence's cell.

"Get up, Romeo," Friar Lawrence said. "Hide yourself."

"No," Romeo said. "I will not be hidden unless the mist from my heartsick groans hides me."

More knocking.

Friar Lawrence said to Romeo, "Listen to the knocking!"

Friar Lawrence shouted, "Who's there? Just a moment!"

To Romeo, he said, "Get up! You will be captured!"

He shouted, "Just a moment!"

To Romeo, he said again, "Get up!"

More knocking.

"Romeo, you are acting like a fool!"

Friar Lawrence shouted, "I'm coming! I'm coming!"

More knocking.

He shouted, "Who is knocking so loudly? From where did you come? What do you want?"

The Nurse, who had been knocking, replied, "Let me come in, and you shall know my errand. Juliet sent me."

Friar Lawrence recognized her voice; she was not a danger to Romeo. He opened the door and said, "Welcome."

The Nurse asked, "Holy friar, tell me: Where is Juliet's husband? Where is Romeo?"

Friar Lawrence replied, "Come in. There he is, lying on the floor, crying. His tears have made him drunk and unable to think well."

"He is acting just like Juliet," the Nurse said. "Their cases of mourning are exactly the same. Both share the same sorrow. Both are in a piteous predicament. Like Romeo, she lies down, blubbering and weeping, weeping and blubbering."

To Romeo, the Nurse said, "Stand up! Stand up! Stand up, if you are a man. For Juliet's sake, rise and stand. Why should you fall into so deep a moan?"

If the ghost of Mercutio had been around, he would have thought, *I wish that I were still alive — the puns I could make! The Nurse talked about a case. A case is a container for holding something. So is a sheath, or vagina. I would make jokes about Romeo being in Juliet's case. The Nurse has talked about rising and standing up for Juliet's sake. I know what part of Romeo should do the rising and standing up. The Nurse talked about Romeo falling into so deep a moan. When people moan, they make an O with their mouths. If I were still alive, I would talk about a different O — Juliet's O between her legs.*

Romeo said, "Nurse!" and stood up.

The Nurse said, "Things could be worse — you could be dead."

"You mentioned Juliet," Romeo said. "How is she? Does she think of me as a hardened murderer now that I have at the beginning of our marriage killed a close relative of hers? Where is she? How is she? What does my secret wife say about our ruined marriage?"

"She does not say anything," the Nurse replied. "All she does is cry and cry. She falls on her bed. She gets up and cries out first the name 'Tybalt' and then the name 'Romeo,' and then she falls on her bed again."

"It is as if my name had been shot from a deadly gun and had murdered her, just as it murdered Tybalt," Romeo said.

He drew his sword and said, "Tell me, Friar Lawrence, in what vile part of my body does my name live? Tell me so that I can cut my name out of myself."

Friar Lawrence said, "Put away your sword. Are you not a man? You look like a man, but your tears make you appear to be womanish. The wildness and lack of thought of your actions make you appear to be an angry beast. You are a shameful woman in the body of a man! Or you are an ugly beast that is half-man, half-woman. You amaze me.

"By my holy order, I thought that you had more sense. You have killed Tybalt. Will you now kill yourself? Don't you know that by killing yourself you would also kill Juliet, your wife, who is now part of you? Why treat yourself with such damnable hatred? Why do you hate your family origin, your soul, and your body? All three of those make up you, and by killing yourself you would lose all three. You are shaming your body, your love, and your mind. Like a usurer who hoards money, you could have good things in abundance, but you do not use your body, your love, and your mind well. Your body should be noble and full of the valor of a man, but you make it seem as if it were made of wax — a sculpture, not a real man. You have sworn to love Juliet, but that must be a lie since by killing yourself you would also kill the person whom you have vowed to cherish. Your intelligence, which should control and manage your body and your love, leads both astray. Your intelligence acts as if it were a stupid soldier who puts gunpowder in a flask and ignorantly sets it on fire. Your intelligence should be used to protect yourself, but instead you are using it to blow yourself up and kill yourself.

"Wise up, Romeo! Your Juliet is alive. To love and marry her, you have risked death! Be happy that Juliet is alive! Tybalt wanted to kill you, but you were able to kill Tybalt. Be happy that you are alive! The law stated that anyone who fought in the streets of Verona would be executed, but instead you are merely exiled. Be happy that Prince Escalus is merciful! You are greatly blessed and happiness has befriended you, but you are acting like a misbehaved and sullen girl — you are pouting despite your good luck and your great love. Be careful because those who are ungrateful die miserable.

"But now, go to Juliet, as was arranged earlier. Climb up to her bedchamber and comfort her. But be careful. Leave before the new set of city guards take up their places in the morning because if you are captured in the morning or afterward you will be killed. Leave earlier so that you can leave Verona and live in Mantua until the time when it is OK to announce publicly your marriage to Juliet, to reconcile the Capulets and the Montagues, and to beg Prince Escalus to pardon you and allow you to live again in Verona. When you return to Verona, you will have twenty hundred thousand times more joy than the lamentation you will endure when you depart from Verona.

"Nurse, go to Juliet first. Give my compliments to her, and tell her to encourage everyone in her father's mansion to go to bed early because of their heavy sorrow. Let her know that Romeo is coming."

The Nurse said to Friar Lawrence, "I could stay here all night and listen to you give advice. To be educated is wonderful!"

She said to Romeo, "I will tell Juliet that you are coming to see her."

"Please do," Romeo said, "and tell her to be ready to speak to me frankly and honestly. I think she will want to know how Tybalt died."

"Romeo, this is a ring that Juliet gave me to give to you," the Nurse said. "Come quickly to Juliet because it is beginning to be very late."

The Nurse departed.

"I feel so much better now!" Romeo said.

"Before you go to Juliet, let me remind you that you need to be gone from Verona before the new set of city guards relieves the guards on duty now," Friar Lawrence said. "The guards on duty now will allow you to leave Verona, but the new guards will arrest you. If you get a late start and the new guards are on duty, you will have to disguise yourself to pass through the gates. Go to Mantua and live there. I will send your servant to you occasionally with news that relates to your situation here — I expect the news to be good. Shake hands with me. It's late. Go to Juliet, and good night."

"A joy that surpasses all joy awaits me," Romeo said, "or else I would be sad at parting from you. Farewell, Friar Lawrence."

69

Old Capulet, Mrs. Capulet, and Paris spoke together in a room in Old Capulet's mansion. Paris loved and greatly desired to marry Juliet.

Old Capulet said to Paris, "Events have occurred that have made it impossible for me to have time to convince Juliet to marry you. As you know, she loved her kinsman Tybalt dearly, as did I. Unfortunately, death is not optional, and anyone who is born will also die. It is very late now, and Juliet will not come down to see you. In fact, I myself should have been in bed an hour ago."

"These times of woe afford no time to woo," Paris said.

To Mrs. Capulet, he said, "Madam, good night. Give my compliments to Juliet."

"I will," Mrs. Capulet said. "And tomorrow morning, I will see how she feels about marrying you. Tonight, she is mourning heavily in her bedchamber."

Old Capulet said, "Sir Paris, I will make a bold offer of my child's love for you. I think that she will do as I advise her to do. In fact, I have no doubt that she will accept my advice."

He said to Mrs. Capulet, "Wife, before you go to bed, go to Juliet and tell her of Paris' love for her. Also tell her that this coming Wednesday — wait, what day is today?"

"Today is Monday, sir," Paris said.

Old Capulet said, "Monday! Well, Wednesday is too soon. So, wife, tell Juliet that she shall marry Paris, my almost son-in-law, on Thursday."

To both Paris and his wife, Old Capulet said, "Will everyone and everything be ready? This leaves little time for preparations, but we should not have too big an affair. Tybalt is very recently dead, and we don't want people to think that we little mourn him. If we have a big affair, they may think that. Therefore, we will have around a half-dozen guests, and that will be enough. But, Paris, what do you think about being married on Thursday?"

Paris replied, "I wish that Thursday were tomorrow."

"Well, go home now," Old Capulet said. "Thursday will be your wedding day, then."

To his wife, he said, "See Juliet before you go to bed, and tell her to prepare for her wedding day."

He then said to Paris, "Good night. I am going to bed. Actually, it is so late that I could almost call it morning. Good night."

Old Capulet knew that Paris loved Juliet and that most young women would be happy to have Paris for a husband. He also knew that Paris, who was related to Prince Escalus, would make a good political ally — especially now that Mercutio and Tybalt had perished because of the feud with the Montagues.

Romeo and Juliet had enjoyed their wedding night together, and now it was almost morning.

Juliet said, "Are you leaving now? It is not yet close to morning. We just now heard the cry of the nightingale and not the morning lark. Each night, the nightingale sings on the pomegranate tree outside. Believe me, Romeo, you heard the cry of the nightingale."

"No, Juliet," Romeo said. "We heard the cry of the lark, the announcer of morning. It was no nightingale. Look, my love, streaks of light reveal the clouds in the East. They announce that for now we must end the happiness of our being together. The stars — the candles of night — have burnt out. The day that makes many people happy now reveals the tops of misty mountains. I must be gone from Verona and live, or stay in Verona and die."

"The light you see is not daylight," Juliet said. "I know that it is not. It is instead the light of one of the shooting stars that will give you light on your way to Mantua, and therefore you need not leave yet."

"Let me be captured and put to death," Romeo joked. "I am happy for that to happen if that is what you want. Just as you wish, I will say that the light I see is not the beginning of dawn. And I will say that the bird I heard so high above our heads is not the morning lark. I have more desire to stay with you than I have will to leave. Come, death, and welcome! Juliet wills it so. Isn't that right, my love? Let us continue to talk — it is not yet dawn."

Realizing that Romeo was in real danger of being killed if he were captured after dawn, Juliet exclaimed, "It is dawn! It is! Leave! Go to Mantua! Do not stay any longer in Verona! It is the lark that sings so out of tune. Its sounds are harsh discords and unpleasing sharps. Some people say that the lark makes sweet divisions — sweet variations on a melody — but the lark does not make sweet divisions because it divides us. Some people believe that because the beautiful lark has ugly eyes and the ugly toad has beautiful eyes, therefore the two must have traded eyes. I wish that the two had traded voices, too. Why should the lark have a beautiful voice when that voice takes us out of each other's arms! It announces that you must leave me now. Oh, leave now and be safe — it grows more and more light!"

"The morning grows more and more light; our woes grow more and more dark," Romeo said.

The Nurse entered Juliet's bedchamber and said, "Juliet, your mother is coming here to speak to you."

The Nurse said to Romeo, "The morning has broken. Beware and be careful. Your life is in danger."

The Nurse left.

Juliet said, "Romeo, climb out through the window, which will all too soon let daylight in."

Romeo said, "Goodbye! One last kiss, and then I will leave."

He kissed her and climbed through the window but did not leave Juliet quite yet.

"You have left me so soon," Juliet said. "Husband, I must hear from you every day in the hour, for in a minute there are many days."

She mourned, "By this way of counting, I shall be very old the next time I see my Romeo."

"Goodbye," Romeo said. "I will omit no opportunity to send my love to you, Juliet."

"Do you think that we shall ever again meet?" Juliet asked.

"I am positive that we will meet again," Romeo replied. "We will tell stories about all of our current troubles to our grandchildren someday."

Romeo climbed down into Old Capulet's garden.

"I have a foreboding of evil," Juliet said. "As I now look down at you, you seem to be like a dead person at the bottom of a tomb. Either my eyesight is playing tricks on me, or you seem pale like a corpse."

"My love," Romeo said, "in my eyes you also seem pale right now. Our sorrows make us appear to be bloodless and so we lose our ruddy hue. Goodbye, Juliet, my wife."

He departed.

"Fortune, people call you fickle," Juliet said. "They say that you are changeable. If you are changeable, what fortune is going to happen to Romeo, who does not change and who is honored for being faithful? I hope that you are fickle, fortune. We have had bad fortune, and good fortune will not keep Romeo long away from me but will bring him back to me quickly."

Mrs. Capulet called, "Juliet, are you awake and up?"

"Who is calling me?" Juliet said to herself. "Is it my mother? Has she not gone to bed tonight, or is she up very early? It is unusual for her to be up and talking to me so early. She must have something important to say to me."

Mrs. Capulet entered Juliet's bedchamber and asked, "How are you, Juliet?"

"I am not well."

"Are you continuing to cry for Tybalt's death?" Mrs. Capulet asked. "Are you trying to wash him from his grave with your tears? Even if you could do that, you would not be able to make him live again. Therefore, stop crying. Some grief shows that you love him, but excessive grief shows a lack of good sense."

"Please let me cry for such a loss I feel with all my heart," Juliet said.

"If you cry, you will feel the loss bitterly, but you will not bring back the person for whom you are crying."

"Mother, I feel the loss so bitterly that I must cry."

"Juliet, I think that you are crying not so much over your cousin Tybalt as you are over the fact that the villain who killed Tybalt is still alive."

"What villain?"

"Romeo."

Juliet said, "The villain and he are many miles apart. God pardon him! I do, with all my heart. And yet no man like he does grieve my heart."

Mrs. Capulet understood this to mean, "The villain Romeo and Tybalt are many miles apart. God pardon the late Tybalt! I do, with all my heart. And yet no man so much as Tybalt does grieve my heart because he has died."

But Juliet knew that to herself, her ambiguous words meant, *The word "villain" and Romeo are many miles apart — Romeo is not a villain! God pardon Romeo! I do, with all my heart. And yet no man so much as Romeo does grieve my heart because he is banished from Verona and my presence.*

Mrs. Capulet said, "You should say, 'And yet no man so much as Romeo does grieve my heart because he is still alive.'"

Juliet said, "I grieve because Romeo is far from the reach of these my hands. I wish that no one but I might avenge Tybalt's death!"

Mrs. Capulet understood these words to mean that Juliet would like to kill Romeo, but she grieves because he is no longer in Verona and so she cannot kill him.

But Juliet knew that to herself, her ambiguous words meant, *I grieve because I can no longer see Romeo, and I would like to be the only person who could avenge Tybalt's death against Romeo because then Romeo would be safe and in no danger.*

Mrs. Capulet said, "Don't worry. We will have vengeance for the death of Tybalt, so you need not cry because Tybalt's death has not been avenged. I am going to send a man to Mantua, where the exiled scoundrel Romeo is said to be fleeing. The man I send to Romeo will give him a drink so poisonous that very quickly Romeo will keep Tybalt company in death. Then, I hope, you will be happy."

Juliet said, "Indeed, I never shall be satisfied with Romeo, until I behold him ... dead ... is my poor heart for a kinsman vexed. Mother, if you could find a man to bear a poison, I would temper it, so that Romeo should, upon receipt thereof, soon sleep in quiet. Oh, how my heart hates to hear him named, and cannot come to him to wreak the love I bore my cousin upon the body of the man who slaughtered him!"

Juliet again used ambiguous words, some of which had two meanings.

This is what Mrs. Capulet heard: "Indeed, I never shall be satisfied with Romeo, until I behold him dead — dead is my poor heart for a kinsman [Tybalt] vexed. Mother, if you could find a man to bear a poison, I would temper [mix] it, so that Romeo should, upon receipt thereof, soon sleep in quiet [die]. Oh, how my heart hates to hear him named, and cannot come to him to wreak [avenge] the love I bore my cousin upon the body of the man who slaughtered him!"

But Juliet knew that to herself, her ambiguous words meant, *Indeed, I never shall be satisfied with Romeo, until I behold him — dead is my poor heart for a kinsman [Romeo] vexed. Mother, if you could find a man to bear a poison, I would temper [weaken] it, so that Romeo should, upon receipt thereof, soon sleep in quiet [take a nap]. Oh, how my heart hates to hear him named, and cannot come to him to wreak [give expression to] the love I bore my cousin upon the body of the man who slaughtered him!*

"You get the poison, and I'll get a man to give it to Romeo," Mrs. Capulet said. "But right now I have good news for you, girl."

"Good news is welcome in such joyless times as these," Juliet said. "What is your good news?"

"You have a father who loves you," Mrs. Capulet said. "He knows that you have been grieving, and to take away your sadness he gives you a day of joy — a day that neither you nor I expected."

"What day is that?"

"Early Thursday morning, a gallant, young, and noble gentleman, Count Paris, at Saint Peter's Church, will happily make you a happy bride."

Shocked, Juliet replied, "By Saint Peter's Church and by St. Peter, too, he will not make me there a joyful bride! I wonder at this haste — why must I wed before I am wooed? Mother, I beg you to tell my father that I will not marry yet; and, when I do marry, I swear that my groom shall be Romeo, whom you know I hate, rather than Paris. Your news is shocking, not joyful."

Her mother told her, "Here comes your father; tell him so yourself, and see how he will take it."

Old Capulet and the Nurse entered Juliet's bedchamber.

Looking at Juliet, who was crying, Old Capulet said, "When the Sun sets, the air drizzles dew. But now, for the sunset of Tybalt, my brother's son, it rains downright."

He said to Juliet, "Your eyes are the source of conduits. Still in tears? Is your face forever showering? With your body you are imitating a ship, a sea, and a wind. Your eyes, like a sea, ebb and flow with tears. Your body is a ship sailing in this salt flood of tears. Your sighs are the winds. Your sighs and your tears — which never cease — will sink your storm-tossed body."

To his wife, he asked, "What is going on here? Haven't you told our daughter about her upcoming marriage to Paris?"

"I have indeed, but she won't have it. She says thanks, but no, thanks. I wish the fool were married to her grave!"

"Let me make sure I understand what you are saying," Old Capulet said. "She refuses to be married and she refuses to thank us for arranging such a splendid marriage? Isn't Juliet elated to marry Paris? Doesn't she realize how blessed she is to have so worthy a gentleman to be her bridegroom? Doesn't she realize that she is unworthy of such a splendid marriage?"

"I am not pleased that you have arranged a marriage for me," Juliet said, "but I am thankful that you have arranged a marriage for me out of your love for me. I hate the marriage that you have arranged for me, but I am thankful for what I hate because I know that you arranged the marriage for me because you love me."

"What are you saying?" Old Capulet said. "You are not making sense: 'Thanks, but no thanks'? Girl, thank me no thankings, but know that on Thursday you and Paris will go to Saint Peter's Church and know that there will be a wedding. Fettle your limbs for a wedding, girl. We fettle — that is, groom — a horse. Like a horse, your limbs will be ridden. If you can't force yourself to go to church, I can force you to go. If I have to, I will drag you there on a hurdle just as if I were taking you to an execution — your execution, you pale-faced girl!"

Knowing that her husband had gone too far, Mrs. Capulet said to him, "Are you insane?"

Juliet said, "Father, I beg you on my knees to listen patiently to what I have to say."

Old Capulet was not in a listening mood: "Headstrong, disobedient girl! I'll tell you what! Either go to church and get married on Thursday, or never after see me! Speak not! Reply not! Do not answer me! I want to slap you!"

To his wife, he said, "We hardly thought that we were blessed to have only one child left living, but now I see that this one is one too many. We are cursed in having her for our daughter! She is worthless!"

The Nurse said to Old Capulet, "God in Heaven bless her! You are to blame, my lord, for criticizing her so."

"And why am I at fault, my lady wisdom?" Old Capulet said. "Hold your tongue, my lady prudence. If you want to say something, go and gossip with your friends!"

"I speak no treason," the Nurse replied.

"Bull!" Old Capulet said.

"May not one speak?"

"Peace, you mumbling fool! Share your wisdom with your friends — but here and now, shut up!"

Mrs. Capulet told her husband, "You are too angry. You are overreacting."

"Damn!" Old Capulet said. "I have a right to be angry! During day and night, during hour and season, during work and play, and alone or among company, I have been doing my best to get Juliet a good husband. Now I have found for her a gentleman of noble parentage, with wealthy estates, youthful, and well connected, handsome and with a manly figure. But what happens! My daughter acts like a wretched, whimpering fool! She acts like a whining, mentally feeble puppet! An excellent groom is handed to her, and she replies, 'I will not marry him. I cannot love him. I am too young. Pardon me.'"

He said to Juliet, "If you will not marry Paris, the kind of pardon I will give you is one you will not enjoy. Yes, you will not have to marry Paris, but no, you will not be allowed to eat or live in this house. Eat and live wherever you can — you shall not eat or live here. Think about what I am saying — you know that this is not a joke. Thursday is coming soon. Consider well my words — take them to heart. You are my daughter, and I will marry you to whomever I wish. If you refuse the marriage, then go hang yourself, beg, starve — die in the streets, for all I care! If you refuse the marriage, you will no longer be my daughter. I will not acknowledge that I am your father, and nothing that I own will ever do you good. Believe what I am telling you! I swear that it is the truth!"

Old Capulet left Juliet's bedchamber.

Juliet said, "Can no one pity me and see my grief? Mother, don't cast me aside! Delay this marriage for a month, a week; or, if you do not, make my bridal bed in that dim tomb where Tybalt lies."

"Don't talk to me," Mrs. Capulet said. "I will not speak a word on your behalf. Do whatever you want to do, for I am done with you."

Mrs. Capulet left Juliet's bedchamber.

Juliet said to the Nurse, "How can we stop this marriage! I already have a husband on Earth. Our vow of marriage is recorded in Heaven. How can that vow of marriage end, freeing me to marry again, unless Romeo dies and enters Heaven? Nurse, give me some comfort. Nurse, give me some good advice. Why is Heaven sending such misfortune to me, who am so weak? Talk to me, Nurse. Do you have even one word of comfort for me?"

"Yes, I do," the Nurse said. "I have advice that I hope will comfort you. Romeo has been banished from Verona, and he will never return to claim you as his wife. Even if he were to return, it would be secretly. Since this is the case, I think it is best that you marry Count Paris — oh, he's a lovely gentleman! Romeo is a dishrag compared to him. Not even an eagle has so attractive, so lively, so beautiful eyes as does Paris. I think this second groom surpasses your first groom, but even if he did not, your first groom is dead to you, or at least as good as dead to you. After all, you are here and he is in exile. You are not able to live together as husband and wife."

Juliet asked, "Are you speaking from your heart?"

"Yes, and from my soul, too," the Nurse said.

Juliet realized that no comfort could come to her from the Nurse, who had just advised her to commit bigamy. Better advice might come from Friar Lawrence.

Juliet said, "Amen."

"What?" the Nurse asked.

"You have comforted me marvelously much," Juliet said. "Go and tell my mother that I regret having displeased my father, and so I have left to go to Friar Lawrence so that I may confess my sins and receive absolution."

"Yes, I will do as you say," the Nurse replied. "You are acting very sensibly."

The Nurse left Juliet's bedchamber.

"That damned old woman!" Juliet said. "She is a very wicked fiend! What is her worst sin? To advise me to commit bigamy and be unfaithful to Romeo, my husband? Or to dispraise my husband after she has praised him beyond compare so many thousands of times previously? Go, Nurse. From here on, you and I shall be separate. You will no longer be my confidant. I will go to Friar Lawrence to seek his advice. If I have no other way to stop this marriage, I can commit suicide."

CHAPTER 4: JULIET IS FORCED TO AGREE TO MARRY COUNT PARIS

— 4.1 —

Count Paris had been talking to Friar Lawrence and asking him to officiate at his wedding to Juliet.

Friar Lawrence now said, "On Thursday, sir? The time before the wedding is held is very short."

"This is what Old Capulet wants," Paris said. "However, I admit that I want to be married quickly."

"You say that you don't know what Juliet thinks about being married to you," Friar Lawrence said. "Weddings should not be arranged until *after* the girl has consented to be a bride. I do not like this."

"She has been excessively grieving because of the death of Tybalt," Paris said, "and therefore I have not been able to woo her as I would like to. Venus does not smile in a house of tears. Juliet's father thinks that it is dangerous for her to grieve so immoderately, and he believes that it is best for her to quickly marry because that will stop her tears. She has been staying by herself and grieving, and her father — as do I — believes that if she is around other people and enjoying society that she will stop grieving. That is the reason for our haste in arranging this wedding."

Friar Lawrence thought, *I know of a reason why this wedding ought not to take place quickly.*

He saw Juliet walking toward his cell, and he said aloud, "Here comes the lady herself walking toward us."

Juliet arrived, and Paris said to her, "Happily met, my lady and my wife!"

Politely, but distantly, Juliet replied, "That may be, sir, when I may be a wife."

Paris said, "That 'may be' must be, love, on this coming Thursday."

"What must be shall be," Juliet said.

"That's the truth," Friar Lawrence said.

"Did you come to make your confession to Friar Lawrence?" Paris asked Juliet.

"To answer that, I should confess to you."

"Do not deny to him that you love me."

"I will confess to you that I love him."

"You will also confess to him, I am sure, that you love me."

"If I tell Friar Lawrence that I love you, that will be more trustworthy than if I said it directly to you."

"Poor Juliet," Paris said, "your face is disfigured by the tracks of many tears."

"The tears have done little to disfigure my face because my face was bad enough before I cried."

"By saying that, you wrong your face even more than the tears have wronged it."

"What is true is not slander," Juliet said. "And I have spoken the truth."

"Your face is mine," Paris said, "and you have slandered it."

Thinking of Romeo, Juliet said, "It is true that my face is not my own."

She asked Friar Lawrence, "Do you have time for me to confess, or should I come to you at evening mass and confess afterward?"

Friar Lawrence said to Juliet, "I have time now."

He said to Paris, "I need to be alone with Juliet so I may hear her confession."

"Heaven forbid that I should keep anyone from confessing their sins!" Paris said to Friar Lawrence.

To Juliet he said, "The morning of the day we will be married, I will wake you up with music. Until then, goodbye."

Paris kissed Juliet's cheek, and then he departed.

"Shut the door," Juliet said. "After the door is shut, come and cry with me. I am past hope, past cure, past help!"

"Juliet, I know, of course, why you grieve," Friar Lawrence said. "I can't think of a way to stop or delay the marriage. Your father is determined that you marry Count Paris this Thursday."

Juliet replied, "Don't tell me that you have heard of this marriage unless you can also tell me how to prevent it. You are wise, but if you cannot think of a way to prevent my marriage to Count Paris, then tell me that what I have resolved is wise, and with this dagger I will commit suicide. God joined my heart and Romeo's heart. You joined our hands in marriage. This hand belongs to Romeo, and before my hand shall be joined in marriage to another man or my heart revolt and turn to another man, this dagger shall slay both my hand and my heart. Therefore, Friar Lawrence, out of your years of experience of living, give me helpful advice or a plan — or else this dagger will solve my problem. Give me a plan quickly. If you can come up with no way to stop this marriage, I long to die quickly."

"Wait, Juliet," Friar Lawrence, who was completely opposed to suicide, said. "I do see a way to stop the wedding. You are in a desperate situation, and the way out will require a desperate action. If you are willing to commit suicide rather than marry Count Paris, then it is likely that you will be willing to undergo something similar to death to avoid marrying him. You will have to encounter something like death itself to escape the shame and sin of committing bigamy and being unfaithful to Romeo. If you are willing to do this, I can help you avoid this marriage."

"I am willing to do much to avoid marrying Paris," Juliet said. "I am willing to jump from the top of a tower. I am willing to walk in a road swarming with thieves. I am willing to stand in a nest of serpents. I am willing to be chained to roaring bears. I am willing to be locked alone in a building where human bones are stored and to be covered with reeking leg bones and yellow, jawless skulls. I am willing to go into a newly made grave and hide with a shrouded corpse. All of these things that I have heard about have made me tremble, but I will do any of them without fear or hesitation in order to stay faithful to Romeo, my sweet love."

"In that case, go home, be merry, and tell your parents — falsely — that you agree to marry Paris," Friar Lawrence said. "Today is Tuesday. On Wednesday night, make sure that you are alone in your bedchamber. Do not let the Nurse stay with you. I have a vial for you to take with you when you leave here. When you are in bed tomorrow night, drink the potion inside the vial. Immediately, the potion will get into your veins and stop your pulse without harming you. Your body will be cold, not warm. You will have no breath. You will have no color in your lips and cheeks. Your eyelids will close. All of the parts of your body shall be stiff and stark and cold. You will appear to be dead for forty-two hours. After that time, you will wake up as if from a pleasant sleep. When Paris comes Thursday morning to wake you up, everyone will think that you are dead. Then, as our tradition is, you will be dressed in your best clothing and carried on a bier to the ancient burial vault where all the deceased Capulets and their kin lie. In the meantime, I shall send a letter to Romeo to tell him about our plan, and he shall secretly return to Verona, and he and I will wait in the Capulet burial vault for you to wake up. After you have woken up, Romeo will take you to Mantua. If you do this, you will not have to marry Count Paris. This plan will work as long as you do not let a womanish fear stop you from drinking the potion in the vial."

"Give me the vial!" Juliet said. "Do not talk to me about fear!"

Friar Lawrence gave her the vial and said, "Leave now. Be brave. Be strong. I will send a fellow friar, a friend of mine, to Mantua with a letter for Romeo."

"Love will give me strength! And strength will help me do what I must do!" Juliet said. "Farewell, dear Friar Lawrence."

In Old Capulet's mansion were Old Capulet, his wife, the Nurse, and some servants.

Old Capulet told a servant, "Take this list and invite to the wedding all the people whose names are on it."

The servant left.

Old Capulet, who had changed his mind about having only a few guests to the wedding, told the second servant, "Go and hire for me twenty good cooks."

The second servant said, "All of the cooks shall be good cooks, sir, because I will test them. I will see if they will lick their fingers."

"Why?" Old Capulet asked.

"A cook's cooking gets on his fingers. A cook who cannot lick his own fingers is a bad cook. Therefore, I will not hire for you any cook who cannot lick his own fingers."

"Leave now," Old Capulet said.

The second servant left.

"We are unprepared for this wedding feast," Old Capulet said. "Has Juliet gone to see Friar Lawrence?"

"Yes," the Nurse replied.

"Maybe he can talk some sense into her," Old Capulet said. "She is a peevish and selfish good-for-nothing."

"Here she comes from confession now," the Nurse said. "She looks happy."

"So, my headstrong young daughter," Old Capulet said, "where have you been gadding about?"

"I have been where I have learned to repent my sin of disobeying you," Juliet said, kneeling before her father. "Friar Lawrence told me to obey you and to ask for your forgiveness, which I do. Henceforward I am ever ruled by you and shall be obedient to your wishes."

Old Capulet immediately made up his mind to hold the wedding a day early.

He said, "Send for Count Paris. Tell him that Juliet has agreed to marry him. The wedding will be held tomorrow morning — Wednesday — not on Thursday."

"I met Count Paris at Friar Lawrence's cell," Juliet said. "I gave him what decorous love I could, but I was careful not to step over the boundary of what is modest."

"I am glad," Old Capulet said. "All of this is good. All things are as they ought to be. Stand up now. Let me see Count Paris. Servant, go and bring Count Paris to me. By God, the city of Verona owes this reverend holy friar a great debt."

Juliet said, "Nurse, will you go with me to my bedchamber and help me to choose the clothing and jewelry that I will wear tomorrow for my wedding?"

Mrs. Capulet said, "No, let's have the wedding on Thursday. We can wait that long."

Old Capulet overruled his wife: "Nurse, go with Juliet. We will have the wedding tomorrow, on Wednesday."

Mrs. Capulet said, "We will be unprepared to host a wedding. Already it is almost nighttime."

"Don't worry," Old Capulet said. "I will handle everything, and everything will be done as it ought to be done. Go to Juliet and help her get ready for her wedding. I will stay awake all night. Leave everything to me, and for this once I will do the work of a housewife."

His wife went to Juliet.

Old Capulet said, "Everyone is gone. Well, I will see Count Paris to let him know about tomorrow's wedding. I feel happy now that my wayward girl is obeying me."

In Juliet's bedchamber, Juliet and the Nurse had been picking out the clothing and jewelry that Juliet was supposed to wear at the wedding.

Juliet said, "Yes, this is what I will wear, but Nurse, please let me be alone tonight because I need to make many prayers to ask God to smile upon me and my wedding. As you know, lately I have been rebellious and sinful."

Mrs. Capulet entered the bedchamber and asked, "How is everything going? Do you need my help?"

"No," Juliet said. "We have already picked out the clothing and jewelry that I will wear tomorrow, so please let me be left alone tonight, and let the Nurse stay up with you tonight because I am sure that you will be up all night making preparations for the wedding."

"Good night," her mother said. "Go to bed and rest. You need your sleep."

"Farewell!" Juliet said.

Mrs. Capulet and the Nurse left Juliet's bedchamber.

"God knows when we shall meet again," Juliet said to herself. "I feel a cold fear going through my veins, nearly causing me to faint. It almost freezes the heat of life. I will call for my mother and Nurse to comfort me."

She called, "Nurse!"

Then she said to herself, "Why am I calling for the Nurse? What should she do here? I need to be alone for what I have to do."

Out of a pocket, she took the vial that Friar Lawrence had given to her.

She said to herself, "What if this potion does not work? Will I then be married to Paris tomorrow morning?"

Juliet took out a dagger.

She said, "If the potion does not work, this dagger will stop my marriage. I will commit suicide."

She put the dagger down in a handy place where it was easy to reach.

Juliet then said, "What if this potion is a poison? If my marriage to Romeo is discovered, Friar Lawrence will be in grave trouble. Perhaps he has given me a poison so that I will die and no one will ever hear of my marriage to Romeo. I am afraid that this potion is a poison, and yet I doubt that it is because Friar Lawrence has always been a righteous man."

Juliet then said, "What if, after I am laid in the tomb, I wake up before Romeo comes? That would be terrifying! Won't I suffocate in the tomb where no healthy air comes in? Won't I die before Romeo comes to get me?

"Or, if I continue to live, what will happen when I am surrounded by death and night in a place of terror — a vault, this ancient receptacle of dead bodies, where for many hundreds of years the bones of all my buried ancestors have been placed, this vault where Tybalt, bloody with his wound, newly interred, lies festering in his shroud? What will happen when I wake up in a place inhabited by ghosts at night? Isn't it likely that I, if I should wake before the arrival of Romeo, will smell rotting flesh and perhaps even hear hideous shrieks of ghosts that drive men mad? Isn't it likely that I will become hysterical because of these fearsome things and insanely play with my forefathers' bones? Isn't it likely that I will pluck the mangled Tybalt from his shroud? Isn't it likely that in an insane fit I will grab a relative's bone and use it as a club to dash out my desperate brains? Look! Already I see Tybalt's ghost seeking Romeo, who spitted his body with a rapier! Stop, Tybalt, stop!"

Juliet held up the vial and said, "Romeo, I am doing this for you. This I drink to you."

Juliet drank the potion, which quickly took effect, and she fell back upon her bed.

In Old Capulet's mansion, Mrs. Capulet said to the Nurse, "Take these keys, and bring more spices."

The Nurse replied, "They are calling for dates and quinces in the pastry room."

Old Capulet entered the room and said, "Stir! Stir! Stir! The second cock has crowed, the curfew-bell has rung, and it is very late at night. Look after the baked meats, good Nurse. Don't worry about the cost."

"You are a man trying to do the work of a woman," the Nurse replied. "Go to bed. If you stay up all night, you will be ill tomorrow."

"Nonsense," Old Capulet said. "I have previously stayed awake all night for less important reasons than this wedding, and I have never felt ill because of it."

"Yes, in your day you chased skirts," his wife said. "But I will make sure that you don't chase any more skirts."

Mrs. Capulet and the Nurse left.

"My wife is jealous," Old Capulet happily said.

Some servants entered the room, carrying spits, logs, and baskets.

Old Capulet asked a servant who was carrying baskets, "Now, fellow, what have you got there?"

"Things for the cook, sir," the servant replied, "but I don't know what they are."

That servant left, and Old Capulet said to another servant, "Fetch drier logs. Call Peter, he will show you where they are."

The servant replied, "I have a brain in my head, sir, and I can find the drier logs without troubling Peter."

The servant left.

Old Capulet said, "Well said, servant, but you are, I think, a loggerhead. Good Heavens, it is already morning. Count Paris will soon be here with his musicians to wake up Juliet. Wait! I hear them playing!"

He listened to the music played by Count Paris' musicians as they walked to his mansion, and then he shouted, "Nurse! Wife! Come here! Nurse, I say!"

The Nurse entered the room, and Old Capulet told her, "Go and wake up Juliet and help her dress. I will go and talk to Paris. Hurry! Hurry! The bridegroom has arrived! Hurry!"

The Nurse entered Juliet's bedchamber to awaken her.

She said, "Juliet, wake up! I bet that you are still fast asleep, slugabed. Why aren't you saying something? Well, you should get your rest. Count Paris will make sure that you get little rest tonight. God forgive me for making such a joke! Well, I need to wake you, but if Count Paris were to find you in bed, he would quickly wake you. Am I not right, Juliet?"

The Nurse drew back the curtains that enclosed Juliet's bed and looked at Juliet.

"What!" the Nurse said. "You woke up, got dressed, and went back to bed to sleep some more. Well, wake up again. Juliet, wake up!"

The Nurse touched Juliet, whose body was cold like a corpse, and the Nurse screamed and shouted, "Help! Help! Juliet is dead! Curse the day that I was born! Bring me something to drink! My lord! My lady!"

Mrs. Capulet entered the room, saying, "What is the reason for this noise?"

The Nurse simply cried.

"What is the matter?"

The Nurse pointed to Juliet and said, "Look!"

Mrs. Capulet looked at Juliet, whose face was pale. She touched Juliet's body and felt how cold it was.

Mrs. Capulet said, "My child, my life, wake up, look up, or I will die with you!"

Old Capulet entered Juliet's bedchamber and said, "What is the reason for this delay? Bring Juliet down to meet Paris; he has come for her."

The Nurse said, "She's dead, deceased — she's dead! Curse this day!"

Mrs. Capulet said, "She's dead! She's dead! She's dead!"

Old Capulet said, "Let me see her!" Like the Nurse and his wife, he touched Juliet.

He said, "She is cold. Her blood has stopped moving. Her joints are stiff. Breath and her lips have long been separated. Death lies on her like an untimely frost lies upon and kills the sweetest flower of all those in the field."

The Nurse and Mrs. Capulet cried, and Old Capulet said, "Death took her away to make me cry, but I am so shocked that I cannot cry."

Friar Lawrence and Paris entered the room.

Friar Lawrence asked, "Is the bride ready to go to church?"

Old Capulet said to him, "She is ready to go to church, but she shall never again return home."

He said to Paris, "The night before your wedding day, Death lay with your wife-to-be. There she lies. She was a flower, and Death has deflowered her. Death is my son-in-law. Death is my heir. Death has married my daughter. I will die, and I will leave Death all I have. Death will get my life and my property — Death will get everything."

Paris said, "For a long time I have longed to see this morning, but now that it has arrived, I see something that I have never longed to see."

Mrs. Capulet said, "This day is accursed, unhappy, wretched, and hateful. This hour is the most miserable hour that ever time saw in its ceaseless passage throughout eternity. I had only one child left alive, one child left to love, one child to rejoice in and take solace in, and cruel Death has taken her away from me!"

The Nurse said, "This is a day of sorrow, of lamentation — the worst day that I have ever experienced. Never was seen so black a day as this."

Paris said, "On this day Death has cheated me, made me divorced, wronged me, spited me, slain me! Cruel Death has overthrown and conquered me. The woman I love is dead!"

Old Capulet said, "Death has treated me badly, distressed me, hated me, martyred me, killed me! Death, why did you come now to murder our wedding ceremony? Child, you were my soul and not just my child — and now you are dead! My child is dead! With my child all my joys are buried."

"Restrain your grief," Friar Lawrence said. "Your exclamations of grief do not help. For fourteen years, Heaven and all of you shared this beautiful maiden, but now Heaven has all of her. Juliet is better off in Heaven than she was in this world. You were not able to keep Juliet's body from dying, but Heaven will keep Juliet's soul forever alive. Here on Earth, you wanted Juliet to gain social prestige. You wanted her to advance in society. Well, now she has advanced to Heaven itself — she is above the clouds and now resides in Heaven! So why do you grieve for her? Do you love your child so badly that you grieve when she achieves the highest happiness that anyone can ever achieve? The best marriage is not a marriage that lasts a long time, but a marriage in which one quickly dies because one rises all the sooner to Heaven. Dry your tears, and cover Juliet's body with rosemary and carry her dressed in her best clothing to church. Our foolish human nature makes us cry for our dear Juliet, but our reason tells us that we should rejoice because Juliet is in Heaven."

Old Capulet ordered, "Everything that we prepared for Juliet's wedding, we now must use for Juliet's funeral. Our musical instruments must play melancholy tunes, our happy wedding feast must become a sad burial feast, our happy wedding hymns must become sullen dirges, our bridal flowers must serve as funeral flowers — everything that was to be used for a wedding must now be used for a funeral."

Friar Lawrence said, "Old Capulet, Mrs. Capulet, Paris, and everyone else, prepare for the funeral. You must follow Juliet's corpse to the church. Heaven is frowning on you because of some sin. Do not anger Heaven any further by attempting to go against the will of Heaven."

In another part of Old Capulet's mansion, the musicians were talking among themselves as the Nurse walked through the room.

A musician said, "Well, we might as well put away our musical instruments and go home."

The Nurse said, "That is a good idea. As you know, Juliet is dead and this is a pitiable case."

She left.

"She is right, you know," the musician said. "The case of my musical instrument is in pitiable shape, but it can be mended. The case of the dead Juliet is something that can never be mended."

Peter, the Capulet servant, entered the room and said, "Musicians, please play for me the song 'Heart's Ease.' If you want me to live, play 'Heart's Ease.'"

"Why do you want us to play 'Heart's Ease'?"

Peter replied, "Because my heart is playing 'My Heart is Full of Woe.' Play something that will comfort me and make me feel better."

"This is not a time for playing music," the musician said.

"You will not play for me?" Peter asked.

"No."

"Then I will give you something sound," Peter punned.

"What will you give us?"

"I certainly will not give you sound money, but I will give you something. I will give you sound sarcasm — I will call you a thieving minstrel."

"Then I will call you a lowly servant."

Peter pulled out a dagger and said, "I really do not need this — I have my fists. I will *do re mi* you — I will rain blows on you from low to high. I will treat you like a percussion instrument. I will give you a sound beating. I will make you a sounding board for my fists. Take note of the notes that I will play on you."

None of the musicians felt threatened by the dagger. One look at Peter, and people knew that he was a clown and not a fighter.

The musician said, "If you *do re mi* us, you will be singing for us. Note those notes."

A second musician said, "Please, put away your dagger, and either put away your wit or put your wit on display."

"My wit is my greatest weapon," Peter said, putting away his dagger. "I can use it to defeat you without even using my dagger. Here is a riddle for you: People often talk about 'music with her silver sound.' Why is sound called silver? What answer do you bring, Simon String?"

The first musician replied, "Because silver has a sweet sound."

"It is a pretty answer, but it is wrong," Peter said. "How do you answer my riddle, Hugh Fiddle?"

"People say 'silver sound' because musicians make sounds for silver coins," the second musician said.

"It is an ingenious answer, and very close to being exactly the right answer," Peter said. "And to what answer would take an oath, James Soundpost?"

"I can't think of an answer," James Soundpost said.

"Then you must be the singer," Peter said. "Tenors have enormous cavities in their heads that enable them to sing well. I bet that you can put an egg in your mouth and close it without breaking the egg. It's such a pity that the enormous cavities in their heads leave tenors little room for brains. But here is the answer to my riddle, hey-diddle-diddle: People refer to 'music with her silver sound' because musicians get no gold coins — they get only silver coins — for making sounds."

With that, Peter departed.

The first musician said, "He was more annoying than he was witty."

"Let him go hang himself," the second musician said. "But let's not go home. We can stay here and wait for the mourners to return from the funeral and eat. At least, we'll get a meal."

CHAPTER 5: TRAGEDY, FOLLOWED BY PEACE

— 5.1 —

Romeo, alone on a street in Mantua, said to himself, "If I may trust the truth — if it is not deceiving — of dreams, my dreams foretell good news and happiness for me. My heart is light, and all day I have been floating above the ground with cheerful thoughts — something unusual of late for me. I dreamt that Juliet came and found me dead — it is a strange dream that allows a dead man to be conscious and think! Juliet kissed me and brought me back to life, and when I lived again, I became an emperor. This dream was very joyful and sweet, but it is but a shadow of the joy I will enjoy and sweetness I will taste when I am again with Juliet, my beloved!"

Romeo's servant, Balthasar, who had remained in Verona so that he could bring news to Romeo as needed, rode a horse up to Romeo.

Romeo said, "News from Verona! How are you, Balthasar? Have you brought me a letter from Friar Lawrence? How is Juliet? How is my father? Again, how is Juliet? I ask about her twice because nothing can be ill, if she is well."

Balthasar replied, "Then she is well, and nothing can be ill. Her body rests in the tomb of the Capulets, and her soul lives with angels. I myself attended her funeral and saw her corpse placed in the tomb. Immediately, I rode here to tell you. Pardon me for bringing you such bad news, but I am following your orders to bring you news from Verona, sir."

"Is what you have said true?" Romeo asked. "Then I defy you, stars! I will choose my own fate and make it fact. Balthasar, you know where I live. Get me ink and paper so that I can write a letter, and get fresh horses for us to ride. I will return to Verona tonight."

"I beg you, sir," Balthasar said, "not to act hastily and without patience. Your looks are pale and wild, and they worry me."

"You have nothing to worry about," Romeo said. "Leave me, and do the things I have ordered you to do. Didn't Friar Lawrence write a letter to me and send it to me by you?"

"No, sir."

"It doesn't matter," Romeo said. "Go and get fresh horses. I will be with you soon."

Balthasar left.

Romeo said to himself, "Well, Juliet, I will lie with you — both of us dead — tonight. What is the best way for me to commit suicide? Funny how quickly the means is found for desperate men! I remember seeing an apothecary, a druggist, who lives near here in his shop. He wears tattered clothing, he has beetle brows, and I saw him gathering medicinal herbs. He was very thin — the sharp misery of poverty had worn him to the bones. In his poverty-stricken shop hung a tortoise, a stuffed alligator, and skins of various ill-shaped fishes. On the mostly empty shelves were a few empty boxes, unfired earthen pots, bladders and musty seeds, bits and pieces of packthread and cakes of rose petals that are too old to freshen the air and ought to be thrown away. All these poor things were on the shelves to make a pretense of merchandise. Noting this penury when I first arrived in Mantua, I said to myself, 'If a man should ever need poison — the sale of which in Mantua is punished by immediate death — here lives a miserable wretch who would sell it to him.' My thought then I will put into action now. I have need of poison, and this needy man will sell it to me. If I remember correctly, this is his shop. Today is a holiday, and his shop is shut."

Romeo called, "Apothecary!"

The apothecary came to the door of his shop and said, "Who is calling so loudly?"

"I want to make a purchase," Romeo said. "I see that you are impoverished. Here are forty gold coins — a fortune for you. In return, let me have some poison — fast-acting poison that will disperse itself through all the veins and kill the life-weary taker as violently and quickly as gunpowder is swiftly fired into the air from the womb of a cannon."

"I have such a poison," the apothecary said, "but the law of Mantua punishes with death anyone who sells it."

"You are thin from hunger and full of wretchedness," Romeo replied. "You are close to death, so why are you afraid to die? I look at your cheeks, and I see famine. I look at your eyes, and I see need and oppression. I look at your back, and I see the contempt that people have for you and for your beggary. The world is not your friend, and neither is the law of Mantua. Mantua has no law that will make you rich; it has only a law that will keep you from becoming rich. Therefore, stop being impoverished — break the law and take these forty gold coins."

"My poverty, but not my will, consents."

"I pay your poverty and not your will."

The apothecary handed Romeo a small vial partially filled with poison powder and said, "Add any liquid you want to this vial of poison, and drink it. After you drink it, it will kill you even if you have the strength of twenty men."

Romeo gave the apothecary the forty gold coins and said, "Here is your gold. Gold is a worse poison and kills more people than this so-called poison that the law of Mantua forbids you to sell. I have given you poison. You have not given me poison. Farewell. Buy food, and gain weight."

He turned away and said to himself, "Come, cordial and not poison, go with me to the grave of Juliet, for there I will drink you and you will make me whole by reuniting me with Juliet."

Friar John walked up to Friar Lawrence's cell and called, "Holy Franciscan Friar Lawrence! Are you home?"

Friar Lawrence said, "I recognize your voice, Friar John. Welcome back from Mantua."

He let Friar John into his cell and said, "What news do you bring me from Romeo? Or, if he has written to me, please give me his letter."

"I have news that will disappoint you," Friar John said. "I went to find another Franciscan friar to accompany me during my journey to Mantua and back. He was visiting the sick when I found him. The health officials of Verona arrived, and thinking that my friend and I were in a house that was infected with the plague, quarantined us in the house. Therefore, I was not able to go to Mantua to give Romeo your letter."

"Then who took my letter to Romeo?" Friar Lawrence asked.

"The health officials were so strict that I was unable to find someone to deliver your letter. In fact, I could not even get a messenger to carry the letter to you and give it to you. And so I return to you your letter."

"This is bad luck, indeed!" Friar Lawrence said. "This letter was not trivial but instead was full of important and urgent news. That it was not delivered may do much damage. Friar John, please go and get me an iron crowbar and quickly bring it to me."

"Brother, I will," Friar John said.

He left to find the crowbar.

"I will go to the Capulet tomb alone," Friar Lawrence said. "Romeo will not be present to accompany me. Within three hours, fair Juliet will awake. She will blame me because Romeo has not received news of our plan, but I will write him another letter and send it to him in Mantua. I will keep Juliet in my cell until Romeo reads my letter and comes to Verona to take her with him to Mantua. I pity Juliet: She is a living corpse in a tomb filled with the dead."

In the churchyard where the tomb of the Capulets was located, Paris and his servant arrived that night. They were carrying flowers and a torch.

"Give me the torch," Paris said to his servant. "Go over there and stand. Wait there. Put out the torch because I don't want to be seen. Under the yew trees, lie on the ground so that you are hidden. Keep your ear to the ground so that you can hear anyone who comes here. The ground is loose because of the digging of dirt. The loose dirt will cause people to stumble, and you will hear them. If someone comes, let me know — whistle. Give me those flowers. Go, and do what I have ordered you to do."

Paris' servant thought, *I am afraid to be here in the graveyard, yet I will stay.*

Paris said, "Juliet, sweet flower, with flowers I decorate your bridal bed, which is also your tomb — the canopy of your bridal bed is dust and stones. Each night, I will bedew your tomb with perfume or with my tears purified by my moans of sorrow. Each night, I will decorate your tomb with flowers and I will grieve."

Paris' servant heard someone coming. The servant whistled.

Paris said, "The boy gives warning that something is approaching. Whose cursed foot wanders this way tonight to interrupt my mourning and true love's rite? It is someone with a torch! Night, hide me for a while!"

Romeo and Balthasar entered the courtyard. They did not see Paris or his servant. Balthasar carried a torch, mattock (a tool shaped like a pickax; the two differently shaped ends — adze and chisel — of its head are often used for digging), and iron crowbar.

Romeo said to Balthasar, "Give me that mattock and the iron crowbar."

Then he handed him a letter and said, "Take this letter that I have written, and early in the morning deliver it to my father. Now give me the torch. I order you that no matter what you hear or see, you do not interfere with what I do. I will enter this tomb partly because I want to see Juliet's face."

Thinking that Balthasar might still be suspicious, Romeo then lied, "But the main reason I need to enter this tomb is to take from Juliet's dead finger a precious ring, a ring that I must use in some important business."

He added, "Now, go. But if you are suspicious and return here to spy on me and see what I do, by Heaven, I will tear you into pieces and strew this hungry churchyard with your limbs. I mean it: I can be both savage and wild. I can be more fierce and more determined than hungry tigers or the roaring and dangerous sea."

Balthasar said, "I will be gone, sir, and not trouble you."

"That is the way to show me friendship," Romeo said.

He handed Balthasar some money and said, "Take this. Live, and be prosperous. Farewell, fine fellow."

Balthasar walked away a short distance but thought, *Despite what I said, I will stay here and hide and see what Romeo does. His looks frighten me, and I am afraid of what he may attempt to do.*

Romeo, thinking himself alone and unwatched, said to himself, "Tomb, you detestable mouth, you belly of death, you have swallowed Juliet. I will force your rotten jaws to open, and to spite you, I will fill you with more food."

Romeo used his tools to open the tomb.

Watching, Paris recognized Romeo: "This is that banished haughty Montague, who murdered my Juliet's cousin Tybalt. It is said that Juliet died from the shock and grief of Tybalt's death. Now Romeo has come here to do some villainous shame to the bodies of Juliet and Tybalt. I will stop him."

Paris stepped out of the shadows that had hid him and said to Romeo, "Stop, vile Montague! Tybalt and Juliet are dead. Can you wreak vengeance even past their deaths? Condemned and exiled villain, I arrest you. Go with me, for you must die."

"I know that I must die," Romeo said. "That is why I came here. Good gentle young man, leave me, a desperate man, alone. Go. Leave me. Think of the dead bodies in this tomb, and let them frighten you so that you dare not stay here. I beg you, don't make me kill you so that I am guilty of another sin. Don't make me angry! Go. By Heaven, I swear that I love you better than I love myself. I have come here bearing a weapon that I will use against myself. Do not stay here. Go, and live, so that you may say, 'A merciful madman begged me to run away.'"

"I defy you and your threats, and I arrest you. You are a felon here in Verona."

"Do you defy me? Then let us fight, boy!"

Romeo and Paris fought.

Paris' servant saw them and thought, *I will go and call the guards.*

He ran out of the courtyard.

Romeo stabbed Paris, who said, "I am dying!"

Paris fell and said to Romeo, "If you are merciful, carry me into the tomb and lay me near Juliet."

Paris died, and Romeo said, "I will do as you ask and place you in the tomb of the Capulets. But I wonder who you are."

Romeo looked at him carefully and said, "So you are Mercutio's cousin, Count Paris. I think Balthasar mentioned you as we rode back to Verona, although I paid little attention to him. I think he said that you were going to marry Juliet. I think Balthasar said that, or perhaps I dreamed it. Or have I become insane and invented the tale because you mentioned Juliet? You are misfortunate like me. I will bury you in this magnificent tomb. A tomb? No, I will bury you in a lantern. Juliet's body lies here, and her beauty makes this tomb a chamber that is full of light."

Romeo carried Paris' body into the tomb and put it down, saying, "Lie there. You are a dead man who has been interred in a tomb by a soon-to-be dead man."

Romeo paused, and then he looked at Juliet and said, "How often are men merry when they are soon to die! Their doctors call such merriment the lightening before death. But how can I call what I am feeling now a lightening? Juliet! My love! My wife! Death had the power to suck away the honey of your breath, but Death does not yet have the power to take away your beauty. Death has not conquered your beauty. Your lips and your cheeks are still red, and Death has not yet planted his pale flag there — the banner of your beauty still flies."

Romeo looked at another body in the tomb and said, "Tybalt, are you lying there in your bloody shroud? What better thing can I do for you than to use the hand that killed you in your youth to kill myself, who was your enemy? Forgive me for killing you, Tybalt!"

Looking again at Juliet, Romeo said, "Why are you yet so beautiful? Should I believe that Death, which has no body, falls in love? Should I believe that Death, that lean, abhorred monster, keeps you here in the dark tomb to be his lover? Because I am jealous of Death, I will always stay with you, and I will never depart from this palace of dim night. Here I will remain with the worms that are your chambermaids. Here I will set up my everlasting rest and end the ill fate that unfavorable stars have brought to my world-wearied flesh. Eyes, look your last at Juliet! Arms, take your last embrace of Juliet! Lips — the gates of breath — seal with a rightful kiss an everlasting contract with brutish Death!"

Romeo kissed Juliet, and then he took out of a pocket the poison that he had mixed with water.

Romeo said, "Poison, you shall be my bitter and unpleasant guide to death! Now I — a desperate pilot — will wreck on rocks that sea-weary ship that is my body! Here's to my love!"

Romeo drank the poison and said, "Apothecary, you spoke the truth: Your poison is quick."

He died.

A little later, Friar Lawrence entered the courtyard, carrying a lantern, a crowbar, and a spade. He walked toward the tomb and said, "Saint Francis, help me! All too often tonight, I have stumbled over graves — a bad omen!"

He heard someone and said, "Who's there?"

Balthasar answered, "A friend — I know you very well."

"May God make you happy!" Friar Lawrence said. "Tell me, friend, whose torch is it that burns dimly among grubs and eyeless skulls. It seems to be burning in the tomb of the Capulets."

"That is correct," Balthasar said. "The torch belongs to a person you know and love."

"Who is it?"

"Romeo."

"How long has he been there?"

"At least half an hour."

"Go with me to the tomb," Friar Lawrence said.

"I dare not, sir. Romeo does not know that I am here. He thinks that I have departed, and he threatened to kill me if I stayed here and spied on him."

"Stay here, then," Friar Lawrence said. "I will go into the tomb alone. Fear comes upon me; I am afraid that some ill, unlucky thing has happened. I am much afraid."

"I think I fell asleep under this yew tree," Balthasar said. "I think I dreamed that Romeo and another man fought and that Romeo killed him."

As he walked to the tomb, Friar Lawrence called, "Romeo!"

Holding his torch, he looked around and said, "Whose blood is this that stains the stony entrance of this tomb? To whom belong these gory swords that lie discolored with red by this place of peace?"

He walked into the tomb and called, "Romeo!"

He looked around, saw Romeo's corpse, and said, "Romeo, you are pale and dead as you lie by Juliet! Who else is here? Paris! You are dead and steeped in blood, Paris! An unkind hour has witnessed this cruel turn of the wheel of fortune."

Juliet moved and Friar Lawrence said, "She awakes."

Juliet sat up, recognized Friar Lawrence, and said, "Comforting friar, where is Romeo? I remember well our plan, and I am in the tomb and awake, as we planned. Where is my Romeo?"

A noise sounded from outside the tomb. Paris' servant had gotten the city guards and was leading them to the tomb of the Capulets.

"I hear some noise," Friar Lawrence said. "Juliet, come from this nest of death, contagion, and unnatural sleep. A greater power than we can resist has thwarted our plan. Come, come away from here. Your husband lies — dead — beside you. Near you, Paris also lies dead. Come with me. I will arrange for you to join a sisterhood of holy nuns. Don't ask me questions now, but leave at once because the city guards are coming. Come with me, Juliet. Let us flee!"

More noise was heard.

Panicked, Friar Lawrence said, "I dare no longer stay!"

Juliet said, "Leave, if you must, but I will not flee from here."

Friar Lawrence ran out of the tomb.

Juliet turned toward Romeo and said, "What is this? A vial enclosed in my true love's hand? It is poison that has caused his death. Romeo, have you drunk it all and left me no friendly drop to drink so I can follow you in death? I will kiss your lips and hope that some poison — a restorative that will restore me to you — is on them to make me die."

She kissed Romeo and said, "Your lips are warm."

A guard outside shouted at Paris' servant, "Lead on, boy! Which way do we go?"

"The noise grows closer," Juliet said. "Therefore, I will die quickly."

She took a dagger from Romeo's belt, "Oh, opportune dagger, my body is your sheath!"

She stabbed herself and said, "Rust there, and let me die."

She fell across Romeo's body and died.

Some city guards and Paris' servant stood outside the tomb.

"This is the place," Paris' servant said. "Look there, where the torch is burning."

The head guard said, "The ground here is bloody. Some of you guards search the courtyard and arrest anyone you find."

He entered the tomb and said, "Here lies Count Paris dead. Here also lies Juliet, bloody, warm, and newly dead, although she has been lying in this tomb for two days."

The head guard looked at the corpse of Romeo and then ordered, "Guards, some of you run and inform Prince Escalus, the Capulets, and the Montagues. Others, search the tomb. We see the ground where all these woes lie, but we cannot know the true ground or cause of all these woes until we know more details."

The head guard went outside the tomb, and some guards arrived with Balthasar in their custody. A guard said, "Here is Romeo's servant. We found him in the churchyard."

"Keep him in your custody until Prince Escalus arrives and investigates what has happened."

Other guards arrived with Friar Lawrence in their custody.

A guard said, "Here is a friar who trembles, sighs, and weeps. We took this mattock and this spade from him as he was leaving this churchyard."

"That is suspicious," the head guard said. "Keep him in your custody."

Prince Escalus and his bodyguards arrived.

"What outrage has occurred that calls me out of bed?" Prince Escalus said.

Old Capulet, Mrs. Capulet, and other people arrived.

Old Capulet asked, "What has happened that causes such noise in the streets?"

Mrs. Capulet said, "Some people in the street cry 'Romeo,' other people cry 'Juliet,' and some other people cry 'Paris.' But all run, shouting, to the tomb of us Capulets."

"Why is everyone shouting?" Prince Escalus asked.

The head guard said, "Sir, here lies Count Paris dead. Here lies Romeo dead. And here lies Juliet, who we had thought was dead two days ago, warm and newly dead."

"Let us find out how all this happened," Prince Escalus said.

The head guard said, "Here are a friar and Romeo's servant. With them are tools that can be used to open a closed tomb."

Old Capulet had entered the tomb and looked at his daughter's body. He returned and told his wife, "Juliet has bled much recently. The dagger in her body is in the wrong place — it should have been found in the back of Romeo."

Mrs. Capulet said, "As a parent, I should have died before my daughter. Older people should die before younger people. Before Juliet died, a funeral bell should have tolled for me."

Old Montague and others arrived.

Prince Escalus said to Old Montague, "Come here. You are up early, and now you will see your son and heir down early this night and early in his all-too-short life."

Old Montague replied, "My liege, my wife died earlier tonight from grief caused by the exile of our son, Romeo. What further grief has now come to harass me in my old age?"

"Look and you shall see."

Old Montague looked into the tomb and saw Romeo, his son, dead.

He cried, "Romeo, what foul manners are these! To die and go into a tomb before your aged father dies!"

"Restrain your cries of grief," Prince Escalus said, "until we find out truly what has happened and why it happened. Then you and I shall both grieve. Two of my relatives — Mercutio and Paris — are dead, and perhaps you and I will both die of grief. I may even die of grief first. In the meantime, restrain your cries of grief and let your head control your heart."

Prince Escalus then ordered, "Bring forth the people you have arrested."

The guards brought forth Friar Lawrence and Balthasar.

Friar Lawrence said, "I am the man who is under the greatest suspicion, and I am the one who is least able to exonerate myself because of the time when and the place where I was arrested. Those place me here at the time of this tragedy. I will both accuse myself and exonerate myself. I will tell you what I have done, and I will tell you my motives in doing what I have done."

"Tell us at once everything you know," Prince Escalus ordered.

"I will be brief," Friar Lawrence said. "The brief time that I may have left to live will not permit a long story. Romeo, who lies here dead, was married to Juliet, who also is lying here dead. I married them. The day of their marriage was also the day of death for Tybalt, whose premature death resulted in banishment for the newly married Romeo from Verona. Juliet mourned, but she mourned for Romeo, not for Tybalt. You, Old Capulet, wanted to stop Juliet's mourning, and so you decided — against her will — to marry Juliet to Count Paris. Wild and distraught, Juliet then came to me and begged me to form a plan that would stop her marriage to Count Paris — or else she would kill herself immediately in my cell. Therefore, I gave her a sleeping potion, which had the effect I intended, for it made her appear to be dead. In the meantime, I wrote a letter to Romeo to tell him to come to Verona this awful night to help me to take Juliet from this tomb at the time she woke up. But the man who was supposed to carry my letter to Romeo in Mantua was forced by circumstances to stay here in Verona and so yesterday he returned to me my letter. All alone this night, I came to take Juliet from the tomb, intending to keep her hidden in my cell until I could find a good time to send news to Romeo. But when I came here tonight, a few minutes before Juliet woke up, here I saw lying dead the noble Paris and faithful Romeo. Juliet awoke, and I begged her to leave the tomb and bear this work of Heaven with patience, but I heard a noise and was frightened and so I left, but Juliet — a desperate woman — would not go with me, and, it appears, she committed suicide. This is what I know. The Nurse can vouch that Romeo and Juliet were married. If any of these cruel events were caused by me, then let my old life end before my time of natural death in accordance with the letter of your law."

"You have a good reputation," Prince Escalus said. "I have always known you to be a righteous man."

He asked the head guard, "Where is Romeo's servant? Let's hear what he has to say."

Balthasar said, "I brought Romeo news of Juliet's death, and he rode a horse here from Mantua to this tomb. I am holding in my hand a letter that he earlier told me to give to his father. He threatened me with death if I did not depart and if I interfered with him, and then he went into the tomb. I decided to stay here, but I did not go into the tomb."

"Give me the letter," Prince Escalus said. "I will read it."

He then asked, "Where is Count Paris' servant — the one who alerted the guards?"

Count Paris' servant was brought before the Prince, who asked him, "What was Count Paris doing here?"

"He came with flowers with which to strew Juliet's resting place," the servant said. "He ordered me to stay at a distance, and I obeyed. Soon someone came with a torch and began to open the tomb. Count Paris drew his sword and they fought, and I ran away to get the guards."

Count Escalus, who had been reading Romeo's letter to his father by the light of torches, said, "This letter provides evidence that shows that Friar Lawrence spoke the truth. Romeo tells of his and Juliet's love for each other. Romeo states that he thought that Juliet was truly dead. And Romeo writes that he bought poison from an impoverished apothecary and came to the tomb of the Capulets to die, and to lie beside Juliet."

Prince Escalus then asked, "Where are these enemies? Capulet! Montague! See what a scourge is laid upon your hate — Heaven has found a way to kill your joys, your children, with love. I have treated your quarrels and battles too softly, and because of my lenience, I have lost two kinsmen: Mercutio and Paris."

He shouted, "All of us are punished!"

Old Capulet said to Old Montague, "Brother, give me your hand. Now that our children, who were married to each other, are dead, we ought to make peace. That is the least that we can do."

"I can do something more for you," Old Montague said. "I will have made a statue of Juliet in solid gold. As long as Verona is called by the name Verona, no one shall be valued more than true and faithful Juliet."

"As rich a statue shall I have made of Romeo, and he will be by Juliet's side. Those two gave their lives because of our former hatred of each other."

Prince Escalus said, "Peace has come to us on this cloudy and grey morning. The Sun, for sorrow, will not show his head. Let us leave here and talk more about these sad events. Some people shall be pardoned, and some people shall be punished, for never was a story of more woe than this of Juliet and her Romeo."

APPENDIX A: ABOUT THE AUTHOR

It was a dark and stormy night. Suddenly a cry rang out, and on a hot summer night in 1954, Josephine, wife of Carl Bruce, gave birth to a boy — me. Unfortunately, this young married couple allowed Reuben Saturday, Josephine's brother, to name their first-born. Reuben, aka "The Joker," decided that Bruce was a nice name, so he decided to name me Bruce Bruce. I have gone by my middle name — David — ever since.

Being named Bruce David Bruce hasn't been all bad. Bank tellers remember me very quickly, so I don't often have to show an ID. It can be fun in charades, also. When I was a counselor as a teenager at Camp Echoing Hills in Warsaw, Ohio, a fellow counselor gave the signs for "sounds like" and "two words," then she pointed to a bruise on her leg twice. Bruise Bruise? Oh yeah, Bruce Bruce is the answer!

Uncle Reuben, by the way, gave me a haircut when I was in kindergarten. He cut my hair short and shaved a small bald spot on the back of my head. My mother wouldn't let me go to school until the bald spot grew out again.

Of all my brothers and sisters (six in all), I am the only transplant to Athens, Ohio. I was born in Newark, Ohio, and have lived all around Southeastern Ohio. However, I moved to Athens to go to Ohio University and have never left.

At Ohio U, I never could make up my mind whether to major in English or Philosophy, so I got a bachelor's degree with a double major in both areas, then I added a Master of Arts degree in English and a Master of Arts degree in Philosophy. Yes, I have my MAMA degree.

Currently, and for a long time to come (I eat fruits and veggies), I am spending my retirement writing books such as *Nadia Comaneci: Perfect 10*, *The Funniest People in Dance*, *Homer's* Iliad: *A Retelling in Prose*, and *William Shakespeare's* Othello: *A Retelling in Prose*.

By the way, my sister Brenda Kennedy writes romances such as *A New Beginning* and *Shattered Dreams*.

APPENDIX B: SOME BOOKS BY DAVID BRUCE

Retellings of a Classic Work of Literature

Arden of Faversham: *A Retelling*

Ben Jonson's The Alchemist: *A Retelling*

Ben Jonson's The Arraignment, or Poetaster: *A Retelling*

Ben Jonson's Bartholomew Fair: *A Retelling*

Ben Jonson's The Case is Altered: *A Retelling*

Ben Jonson's Catiline's Conspiracy: *A Retelling*

Ben Jonson's The Devil is an Ass: *A Retelling*

Ben Jonson's Epicene: *A Retelling*

Ben Jonson's Every Man in His Humor: *A Retelling*

Ben Jonson's Every Man Out of His Humor: *A Retelling*

Ben Jonson's The Fountain of Self-Love, or Cynthia's Revels: *A Retelling*

Ben Jonson's The Magnetic Lady, or Humors Reconciled: *A Retelling*

Ben Jonson's The New Inn, or The Light Heart: *A Retelling*

Ben Jonson's Sejanus' Fall: *A Retelling*

Ben Jonson's The Staple of News: *A Retelling*

Ben Jonson's A Tale of a Tub: *A Retelling*

Ben Jonson's Volpone, or the Fox: *A Retelling*

Christopher Marlowe's Complete Plays: Retellings

Christopher Marlowe's Dido, Queen of Carthage: *A Retelling*

Christopher Marlowe's Doctor Faustus: *Retellings of the 1604 A-Text and of the 1616 B-Text*

Christopher Marlowe's Edward II: *A Retelling*

Christopher Marlowe's The Massacre at Paris: *A Retelling*

Christopher Marlowe's The Rich Jew of Malta: *A Retelling*

Christopher Marlowe's Tamburlaine, Parts 1 and 2: *Retellings*

Dante's Divine Comedy: *A Retelling in Prose*

Dante's Inferno: *A Retelling in Prose*

Dante's Purgatory: *A Retelling in Prose*

Dante's Paradise: *A Retelling in Prose*

The Famous Victories of Henry V: *A Retelling*

From the Iliad *to the* Odyssey: *A Retelling in Prose of Quintus of Smyrna's* Posthomerica

George Chapman, Ben Jonson, and John Marston's Eastward Ho! *A Retelling*

George Peele's The Arraignment of Paris: *A Retelling*

George Peele's The Battle of Alcazar: *A Retelling*

George's Peele's David and Bathsheba, and the Tragedy of Absalom: *A Retelling*

George Peele's Edward I: *A Retelling*

George Peele's The Old Wives' Tale: *A Retelling*

109

George-a-Greene: *A Retelling*

The History of King Leir: *A Retelling*

Homer's Iliad: *A Retelling in Prose*

Homer's Odyssey: *A Retelling in Prose*

J.W. Gent.'s The Valiant Scot: *A Retelling*

Jason and the Argonauts: A Retelling in Prose of Apollonius of Rhodes' Argonautica

John Ford: Eight Plays Translated into Modern English

John Ford's The Broken Heart: *A Retelling*

John Ford's The Fancies, Chaste and Noble: *A Retelling*

John Ford's The Lady's Trial: *A Retelling*

John Ford's The Lover's Melancholy: *A Retelling*

John Ford's Love's Sacrifice: *A Retelling*

John Ford's Perkin Warbeck: *A Retelling*

John Ford's The Queen: *A Retelling*

John Ford's 'Tis Pity She's a Whore: *A Retelling*

John Lyly's Campaspe: *A Retelling*

John Lyly's Endymion, The Man in the Moon: *A Retelling*

John Lyly's Galatea: *A Retelling*

John Lyly's Love's Metamorphosis: *A Retelling*

John Lyly's Midas: *A Retelling*

John Lyly's Mother Bombie: *A Retelling*

John Lyly's Sappho and Phao: *A Retelling*

John Lyly's The Woman in the Moon: *A Retelling*

John Webster's The White Devil: *A Retelling*

King Edward III: *A Retelling*

Mankind: *A Medieval Morality Play* (A Retelling)

Margaret Cavendish's The Unnatural Tragedy: *A Retelling*

The Merry Devil of Edmonton: *A Retelling*

The Summoning of Everyman: *A Medieval Morality Play* (A Retelling)

Robert Greene's Friar Bacon and Friar Bungay: *A Retelling*

The Taming of a Shrew: *A Retelling*

Tarlton's Jests: A Retelling

Thomas Middleton's A Chaste Maid in Cheapside: *A Retelling*

Thomas Middleton's Women Beware Women: *A Retelling*

Thomas Middleton and Thomas Dekker's The Roaring Girl: *A Retelling*

Thomas Middleton and William Rowley's The Changeling: *A Retelling*

The Trojan War and Its Aftermath: Four Ancient Epic Poems

Virgil's Aeneid: *A Retelling in Prose*

William Shakespeare's 5 Late Romances: Retellings in Prose

William Shakespeare's 10 Histories: Retellings in Prose

William Shakespeare's 11 Tragedies: Retellings in Prose

William Shakespeare's 12 Comedies: Retellings in Prose

William Shakespeare's 38 Plays: Retellings in Prose
William Shakespeare's 1 Henry IV, aka Henry IV, Part 1: *A Retelling in Prose*
William Shakespeare's 2 Henry IV, aka Henry IV, Part 2: *A Retelling in Prose*
William Shakespeare's 1 Henry VI, aka Henry VI, Part 1: *A Retelling in Prose*
William Shakespeare's 2 Henry VI, aka Henry VI, Part 2: *A Retelling in Prose*
William Shakespeare's 3 Henry VI, aka Henry VI, Part 3: *A Retelling in Prose*
William Shakespeare's All's Well that Ends Well: *A Retelling in Prose*
William Shakespeare's Antony and Cleopatra: *A Retelling in Prose*
William Shakespeare's As You Like It: *A Retelling in Prose*
William Shakespeare's The Comedy of Errors: *A Retelling in Prose*
William Shakespeare's Coriolanus: *A Retelling in Prose*
William Shakespeare's Cymbeline: *A Retelling in Prose*
William Shakespeare's Hamlet: *A Retelling in Prose*
William Shakespeare's Henry V: *A Retelling in Prose*
William Shakespeare's Henry VIII: *A Retelling in Prose*
William Shakespeare's Julius Caesar: *A Retelling in Prose*
William Shakespeare's King John: *A Retelling in Prose*
William Shakespeare's King Lear: *A Retelling in Prose*
William Shakespeare's Love's Labor's Lost: *A Retelling in Prose*
William Shakespeare's Macbeth: *A Retelling in Prose*
William Shakespeare's Measure for Measure: *A Retelling in Prose*
William Shakespeare's The Merchant of Venice: *A Retelling in Prose*
William Shakespeare's The Merry Wives of Windsor: *A Retelling in Prose*
William Shakespeare's A Midsummer Night's Dream: *A Retelling in Prose*
William Shakespeare's Much Ado About Nothing: *A Retelling in Prose*
William Shakespeare's Othello: *A Retelling in Prose*
William Shakespeare's Pericles, Prince of Tyre: *A Retelling in Prose*
William Shakespeare's Richard II: *A Retelling in Prose*
William Shakespeare's Richard III: *A Retelling in Prose*
William Shakespeare's Romeo and Juliet: *A Retelling in Prose*
William Shakespeare's The Taming of the Shrew: *A Retelling in Prose*
William Shakespeare's The Tempest: *A Retelling in Prose*
William Shakespeare's Timon of Athens: *A Retelling in Prose*
William Shakespeare's Titus Andronicus: *A Retelling in Prose*
William Shakespeare's Troilus and Cressida: *A Retelling in Prose*
William Shakespeare's Twelfth Night: *A Retelling in Prose*
William Shakespeare's The Two Gentlemen of Verona: *A Retelling in Prose*
William Shakespeare's The Two Noble Kinsmen: *A Retelling in Prose*
William Shakespeare's The Winter's Tale: *A Retelling in Prose*